Sergio Ramírez

STORIES

translated by Nick Caistor

readers international

The first six of these stories appeared under the title *Charles Atlas también muere,* first published in Mexico in 1976 and reissued by Editorial Nueva Nicaragua, Managua, 1982. The last two stories appear here for the first time in any collection.

First published in English by Readers International, Inc., London and New York, whose editorial branch is at 8 Strathray Gardens, London NW3 4NY, England. US/Canadian inquiries to Subscriber Service Department, P.O.Box 959, Columbia, Louisiana 71418 USA.

Cover illustration "The Cotton Harvest" by the Nicaraguan artist Miriam Guevara
Design by Jan Brychta
Typeset by Grassroots Typeset, London NW6
Printed and bound in Great Britain by Richard Clay (The Chaucer Press) Ltd., Bungay, Suffolk

ISBN 0-930523-28-8 Hardcover
ISBN 0-930523-29-6 Paperback

Contents

Charles Atlas Also Dies

Charles Atlas swears that sand story is true.
Edwin Pope, Sports Editor,
The Miami Herald

How well I remember Captain Hatfield USMC on the day
he came down to the quayside at Bluefields to see me off
on the boat to New York. He gave me his parting words
of advice, and lent me his English cashmere coat: it must
be cold up there, he said. He came with me to the gangway
and then, after I had clambered into the launch, gave me
a long handshake. As I rode out to the steamer, which stood
well off the coast, I saw him for the last time, a lean, bent
figure in army boots and fatigues, waving me good-bye with
his cap. I say for the last time because three days later he
was killed in a Sandinista attack on Puerto Cabezas, where
he was garrison commander.

Captain Hatfield USMC was a good friend. He taught
me to speak English with his Cortina method records,
played for me every night in the barracks at San Fernando
on the wind-up gramophone. It was he who introduced me
to American cigarettes. But above all, I remember him for
one thing: he enrolled me in the Charles Atlas correspondence course, and later helped me get to New York to see
the great man in person.

It was in San Fernando, a small town up in the
Segovias Mountains, that I first met Captain Hatfield
USMC. That was back in 1926: I was a telegraph operator,

and he arrived in command of the first column of Marines, with the task of forcing General Sandino and his followers down from Mount Chipote, where they had holed up. It was me who transmitted his messages to Sandino and received the replies. Our close friendship, though, started from the day he gave me a list of the inhabitants of San Fernando and asked me to mark all those I thought might be involved with the rebels or had relatives among them. The next day they were all marched off, tied up, to Ocotal, where the Americans had their regional headquarters. That night, to show his gratitude, he gave me a packet of Camels (which were completely unknown in Nicaragua in those days) and a magazine with pin-up photos. It was there I read the ad that changed my whole life, transforming me from a weakling into a new man:

THE 97-POUND WEAKLING
WHO MADE HIMSELF THE WORLD'S
MOST PERFECTLY DEVELOPED MAN

Ever since I was a child, I had suffered from being puny. I can remember how once when I was strolling around the square in San Fernando after Mass with my girlfriend Ethel—I was 15 at the time—two big hefty guys walked past us, laughing at me. One of them turned back and kicked sand in my face. When Ethel asked me, "Why did you let them do that?" all I could find to reply was: "First of all, he was a big bastard; and second, I couldn't see a thing for the sand in my eyes."

I asked Captain Hatfield USMC for help in applying for the course advertised in the magazine, and he wrote on my behalf to Charles Atlas in New York, at 115 East

23rd Street, to ask for the illustrated brochure. Almost a year later—San Fernando is in the midst of the mountains, where the heaviest fighting was going on—I received the manila envelope containing several colored folders and a letter signed by Charles Atlas himself. "The Complete Dynamic Tension Course, the summit in body-building. Simply tell me where on your body you'd like muscles of steel. Are you fat and flabby? Limp and listless? Do you tire easily and lack energy? Do you stay in your shell and let others walk off with the prettiest girls, the best jobs, etc? Give me just seven days and I'll prove that I can turn you too into a real man, full of health, of confidence in yourself and your own strength."

Mr. Atlas also said in his letter that this course would cost a total of thirty dollars. That kind of money was far beyond my means, so again I turned to Captain Hatfield USMC, who presented me with another list of local people, almost all of whom I marked for him. The money was soon sent off, and within the year I had received the complete course of 14 lessons with their 42 exercises. Captain Hatfield took personal charge of me. The exercises took only 15 minutes a day. "Dynamic Tension is a completely natural system. It requires no mechanical apparatus that might strain the heart or other vital organs. You need no pills, special diet, or other tricks. All you need are a few minutes of your spare time each day—and you'll really enjoy it!"

But since I had more spare time than I knew what to do with, I could dedicate myself wholeheartedly to the exercises for three hours rather than fifteen minutes every day. At night I was studying English with Captain Hatfield. After only a month, my progress was astonishing.

My shoulders had broadened, my waist had slimmed down, and my legs had firmed up. Scarcely four years after that big bully had kicked sand in my eyes, I was a different man. One day, Ethel showed me a photo of the mythological god Atlas in a magazine. "Look," she said, "he's just like you." Then I knew I was on the right track and would one day fulfill my dreams.

Four months later, my English was good enough for me to be able to write and thank Mr. Atlas myself: "Everything is OK." I was a new man with biceps of steel, and capable of a feat like the one I performed in the capital, Managua, the day that Captain Hatfield USMC took me there to give a public demonstration of my strength. Dressed in a tiger-skin leotard, I pulled a Pacific Railway car full of chorus girls for a distance of two hundred yards. President Moncada himself, together with the special American envoy Mr. Hanna and Colonel Friedmann, the commander of the Marines in Nicaragua, all came to see me.

Doubtless it was this achievement, which was reported in all the newspapers, that made it easier for Captain Hatfield to forward the application I had made when the two of us left San Fernando: a trip to the United States to meet Charles Atlas in person. Captain Hatfield's superiors in Managua made a formal request to Washington, and just over a year later this was approved. The news appeared in the papers at the time; more precisely, in *La Noticia* for September 18, 1931, I was photographed standing next to the US cultural attaché, a certain Mr. Fox, this being almost certainly the first cultural exchange between our two countries, although they became so common afterwards. The caption read: "Leaving for a tour of physical culture centers in the United States, where he will also meet outstanding personalities from the world of athletics.''

So it was that, following a peaceful crossing with a short call at the port of Veracruz, we arrived in New York on November 23, 1931. I must confess that, as the ship berthed, a feeling of great desolation overwhelmed me, despite all the warnings Captain Hatfield USMC had given me. From books, photographs, and maps, I had formed a precise image of New York City—but it was a static one. This was torn to shreds by the frenetic movement of animate and inanimate objects around me, and I was plunged into a terrifying fantasy full of invisible trains, a sky blackened by countless chimneys, a stench of soot and sewage, the scream of distant sirens, and a constant rumbling from the earth beneath my feet.

I was met by someone from the State Department, who took care of immigration and drove me to my hotel— the Hotel Lexington to be exact—a huge brick building on 48th Street. He told me everything had been arranged for me to see Mr. Atlas the following morning. I was to be picked up at my hotel and taken to the offices of Charles Atlas, Inc., where everything would be explained to me. With that we said good-bye, as he had to return to Washington the same evening.

It was cold in New York, so I went to bed early, full of an understandable excitement now that I was reaching my journey's end and seeing my greatest ambition fulfilled. I looked out at the infinity of lights from skyscraper windows that sparkled through the fog. Somewhere out there, I thought, behind one of those windows, is Charles Atlas. He's reading, having dinner, sleeping, or talking to someone. Or perhaps he's doing the nightly exercises—

numbers 23 and 24 in the handbook (flexing the neck and wrists). Maybe he has a smile on his fresh, cheerful face beneath hair greying at the temples. Or perhaps he is still busy replying to the thousands of letters he receives every day, and sending off the packages with the handbooks. One thing suddenly occurred to me: I couldn't imagine Charles Atlas with clothes on. I always thought of him in his swimming trunks, with his muscles flexed, but found it impossible to picture him in a suit or hat. I rummaged in my suitcase till I found the signed photograph he had sent me on completion of the course. There he stood, hands cupped behind his head, body slightly arched and his pectoral muscles effortlessly tensed, his legs together, and one shoulder tilted higher than the other. It was beyond me to try and imagine such a body clothed, and the idea was still turning in my mind as I fell asleep.

By five in the morning I was already awake. I carried out exercises 1 and 2 (how thrilling to be doing them in New York for the very first time) and imagined that Charles Atlas was probably performing the same ones right at that moment. I took my shower and dressed as slowly as possible, killing time, but by seven o'clock I was downstairs in the hotel lobby waiting to be picked up as instructed. Although Charles Atlas did not exactly specify it, I never ate breakfast anyway.

At nine o'clock sharp the man from Charles Atlas, Inc., arrived. Waiting for us outside was a black limousine with gold trim on its windows and grey velvet curtains. The escort did not open his mouth once during the whole trip, nor did the chauffeur so much as glance around. We drove for half an hour along streets lined with the same brick buildings, row upon row of windows, and always the dull daylight between the skyscrapers as though it was about to rain. The black car finally pulled up in front of the eagerly awaited number 115 on East 23rd Street. It was a depressing street full of warehouses and wholesale depositories. I remember that across from Charles Atlas, Inc., was an umbrella factory and a small park of dusty, withered trees. All the buildings seemed to have their windows boarded up.

To reach the front entrance of Charles Atlas, Inc., we climbed some stone steps up to a small terrace, where a life-sized statue of the mythological god Atlas was carrying the world on his shoulders. The inscription read: *Mens sana in corpore sano*. We went in through a squeaky revolving door of polished glass set in black enamelled frames. The walls of the lobby were covered with huge blow-ups of all the photographs of Charles Atlas I knew so well. What a thrill to recognize each of them in turn: particularly the one in the center, which showed him, a harness around his neck, pulling ten automobiles while a shower of ticker-tape fell about him. Magnificent!

I was shown into the office of Mr. William Rideout. Jr., the general manager of Charles Atlas, Inc. Within a few moments I was joined by a middle-aged man with a gaunt face and eyes sunk deep into dark sockets. He held out a pale hand, on which a mass of blue veins stood out, then sat down behind a small, square desk. He switched on a lamp behind him, though to me this hardly seemed necessary, as the window let in enough light already.

The offices were rather shabby. The desk was littered with piles of letters identical to the one I had received at the start of the course. The wall in front of me was dominated by an enormous photograph (one I had never seen before) of Charles Atlas proudly showing off his pectoral muscles. Mr. Rideout asked me to take a seat, then began to speak without so much as looking up at me. He kept staring at a paperweight on the desk, and had his hands crossed in front of him. It was plain from his expression that he found it a great effort to talk. I was trying so hard to follow his dull monotonous voice that it wasn't until he paused to wipe the corners of his mouth that I noticed something my nervousness had prevented me from seeing before: his clenched hands and lowered head could only mean exercise 18 of the Dynamic Tension System. I must admit I was so moved I came close to tears.

"I welcome you most cordially," Mr. Rideout Jr. had begun, "and I hope you have an enjoyable stay in New York. I'm sorry not to be able to talk proper Spanish with you as I should have wished, but I only speak *un poquito.*" As he said this, he measured out a tiny gap between the thumb and first finger of his right hand, then burst out laughing for the first and only time, as though he had said something tremendously funny.

Mr. Rideout Jr. then beamed at me condescendingly while he straightened his tie. "I am the general manager of Charles Atlas, Inc., and it is a great pleasure for my company to receive you as an official guest of the US State Department. We will do all we can to make your stay here with us a pleasant one." He again dabbed at his lips with the handkerchief, then launched into a longer speech, which gave me the opportunity to observe his aged secretary as she turned down the Venetian blind on the street window, throwing the room into semi-darkness. Its whole appearance changed in an instant, and new objects came to the fore, as if Charles Atlas had suddenly shifted his pose in the many photographs displayed on the walls.

"I'm delighted that you should have come from so far away to meet Charles Atlas, and must confess that this is the first time anything of the kind has happened in the entire history of the company," Mr. Rideout Jr. was saying. "As in any commercial enterprise, we keep to ourselves certain matters which, should they become public knowledge, would only harm our interests. For that reason I must ask you to swear a solemn oath of silence concerning what I am about to tell you."

He repeated the same warning several times, speaking calmly and evenly now. I swallowed and nodded my agreement.

"Swear out loud," he said.

"I swear," I managed to get out.

Although by now we were completely alone in the room, and the only sound was the hum of the radiator, Mr. Rideout Jr. looked all around him before he spoke.

"Charles Atlas doesn't exist," he whispered, leaning over towards me. Then he dropped back into his seat, and stared at me with a grave expression on his face. "I know this must come as a great shock to you, but it's the truth. We invented our product in the last century, and Charles Atlas is a trademark like any other, like the cod fisherman on the Scott's emulsion box or the clean-shaven face on Gillette razor-blades. It's simply what we sell."

During our long talks after the English classes back in San Fernando, Captain Hatfield USMC had often warned me about this kind of situation: never drop your guard. Be like a boxer—don't be taken by surprise. Stand up for yourself. Don't let them fool you.

"Very well," I said, rising to my feet, "I shall have to inform Washington of this."

"What's that?" Mr. Rideout Jr. exclaimed, also getting to his feet.

"Yes, that's right, I'll have to tell Washington about this setback." (Washington is a magic word, Captain Hatfield USMC had taught me. Use it when you're in a tight spot, and if by any chance that doesn't work, hit them with the other, the State Department: that's a knockout.)

"I beg you to believe me. I'm telling you the truth," Mr. Rideout said, but with a faltering voice.

"I'd like to cable the State Department."

"I swear I'm not lying to you..." were his parting words as he backed his way out of the room, closing a narrow door behind him. I was left all on my own in the gloom. If I were to believe Captain Hatfield, the trembling in my legs must be caused by passing underground trains.

It was late afternoon before Mr. Rideout Jr. appeared again. Hammer away, keep hammering at them, I could hear Captain Hatfield USMC advising me.

"I will never believe that Charles Atlas doesn't exist," I said before he had a chance to speak. He crumpled into his chair.

"All right, you win," he conceded, with a wave of his hand. "The firm has agreed for you to meet Mr. Atlas."

I smiled and thanked him with a satisfied nod. Be kind and polite once you know you've won, another of Captain Hatfield USMC's recommendations.

"But you must promise to adhere strictly to the following conditions. The State Department has been consulted, and they have approved the document that you are to sign. You must undertake to leave the country after seeing Mr. Atlas. A passage has been booked for you on the *Vermont*, which sails at midnight. You must also refrain from making any public or private comment on your meeting, and from relating anything that may happen, or your personal impressions, to anyone at all. It is only on these conditions that the board has given its approval.''

The ageing secretary came in again and handed Mr. Rideout a sheet of paper. He pushed it over to me. ''Sign here,'' he said peremptorily.

Without another word, I signed where he was pointing. Once you've got what you want, sign any damn thing apart from your death sentence: Captain Hatfield USMC.

Mr. Rideout Jr. took the document, folded it carefully, and put it in the middle drawer of the desk. Even as he was doing so, I felt myself being lifted from the chair. I looked round and saw two huge muscle-bound men dressed in black, with identical shaven heads and scowls. No doubt their bodies too had been developed thanks to the rigors of the Dynamic Tension System.

''These gentlemen will go with you. Follow their instructions to the letter.'' At that, Mr. Rideout Jr. disappeared once more through the narrow door, without so much as a farewell handshake.

The two men, without ever loosening their grip, led me out into a long corridor, which eventually brought us to a wooden staircase. They barked at me to go down first: by the bottom, I was in complete darkness. One of them pushed past me and knocked on a door. It was opened from the far side by a third man who was the mirror image of my two. We stepped out onto a small concrete landing-stage. I couldn't say for certain where we were, because the fog had come swirling down again, but I'm pretty certain it was the river front, for they led me over to a tugboat, which set off at a snail's pace into the mist. The stench from the refuse barges it was pulling reached us even up in the prow.

Night had fallen by the time we disembarked and continued our way on foot along an alley lined with stacks of empty bottle crates. We pushed our way through circles of black children playing marbles by the light of gas lamps and finally emerged into a square where tufts of withered grass alternated with dirty strips of trampled ice left from a snowfall. In front of us were the backs of four or five dark buildings with their tangled web of fire escapes. The hum of distant traffic and the wail of trains miles away came and went on the smoke-filled air.

Renewed pressure on my arms directed me to one side of the square, and we entered the courtyard of a grim edifice that turned out to be a church, whose dank, acrid-smelling walls were covered in bas-reliefs of angels, flowers and saints. By the light of a match that one of my companions struck to find the door knocker, I managed to read the name on a bronze plaque: Abyssinian Baptist Church. As the booming echoes of the knocker faded in the icy night, the door was opened by another guard, also huge, muscle-bound and tough-looking.

We walked up the main nave to the high altar, then I was pushed towards a door on the left. I was filled with sadness and exhaustion. I felt so unsure of what might happen next that I almost regretted having provoked the situation I now found myself in. Again though, Captain Hatfield USMC's voice raised my spirits: once you're on your way, my boy, never look back.

An old woman in a starched white uniform stood waiting for me. My two friends finally let go of me, and positioned themselves on either side of the door. "You've got precisely half an hour," one of them growled. The aged nurse led the way along a dazzlingly white corridor. Ceiling, walls, all the doors we passed, even the floor tiles were white, while the fluorescent strips only added to this pure, empty light.

The old woman hobbled slowly to a double door at the end of the corridor. One side was open, but the view inside was blocked by a folding screen. With a trembling hand she gestured for me to go in, then vanished. I knocked gently three times, but nobody seemed to have heard the timid rap of my knuckles on the blistered layers of paint that had been daubed repeatedly on the door.

My heart was in my mouth as I knocked once more, determined that if there was no answer this time I would turn back. But suddenly a tall, ungainly nurse with thinning, bleached hair who was also dressed in dazzling white appeared from behind the screen. She gave me a broad, relaxed smile that revealed her perfect horse teeth.

"Come in," she said. "Mr. Atlas is expecting you."

The room was bathed in the same artificial whiteness, the same empty light in which millions of tiny dust particles floated. All the objects in the room were white too: the chairs and a medical trolley piled with cotton wool, gauze, bottles and surgical instruments. The walls were bare, apart from a painting that showed the white naked body of a beautiful young woman stretched out on a table while an ancient surgeon held up the heart he had just cut from her. There were bed pans on the floor, and the windows were covered with blinds that during the day must filter out nearly all the light.

At the back of the room on a raised platform was a

high, jointed bed with a complicated system of levers and springs. I tiptoed slowly towards it, then stopped halfway, almost overcome by the smell of disinfectant. I looked around for one of the white chairs to sit on, but the nurse, who was already beside the bed, beckoned me, smiling, to come forward.

On the bed lay the unmoving apparition of a giant, muscular body, its head buried somewhere among the pillows. When the nurse leaned over to whisper something, the body stirred with difficulty and came upright. Two of the pillows fell to the floor, but as I started to pick them up, she stopped me with her hand.

"Welcome," said a voice that echoed strangely as though through an antiquated megaphone. It brought a lump to my throat—I wished with all my heart I hadn't started this.

"Thank you, thank you so much for your visit," the voice was now saying. "Believe me, I really appreciate it," the words came bubbling out, as though the voice were drowning in a sea of thick saliva. Then there was silence, and the huge body fell back onto the pillows.

I cannot describe my grief. I would have preferred a thousand times to have believed that Charles Atlas was an invention, that he had never existed, than to have to confront the reality that *this* was he. He spoke from behind a gauze mask, but I glimpsed that a metal plate had been screwed in to replace his lower jaw.

"Cancer of the jaw," he gasped, "spreading now to the vital organs. Until I was 95, I had an iron constitution. Now that I'm over a hundred, I can't complain. I've never smoked, and never drunk more than the occasional glass of champagne at Christmas or New Year. I never had any illness worse than a common cold, and the doctor was always telling me, until just recently, that I could have children if I wanted to. When in 1843 I won the title of the world's most perfectly developed man...in Chicago...I remember..." but at this point his voice trailed off in a series of pitiful wheezes, and he remained silent for some time.

"It was 1843 when I discovered the Dynamic Tension System and set up the correspondence courses, on the advice of a sculptress, Miss Ethel Whitney, who I used to pose for as a model."

Then Charles Atlas lifted his enormous arms from under the sheets. He flexed his biceps and cupped his hands behind his head. In doing so he dislodged the bed covers so that I caught sight of his torso, still identical to the photos, apart from the white fuzz on his chest. It must have cost him a great effort, because he began to moan, and the nurse rushed to his side. She pulled the sheets back up, and adjusted the plate on his jaw.

"I was 14 years old when I left Italy with my mother," he went on. "I had no idea then that I was going to make a fortune with my courses. I was born in Calabria in 1827. My real name is Angelo Siciliano; my father had come to New York a year earlier and we followed him. One day when I was at Coney Island with my girl friend, a big bully kicked sand in my face, so I..."

"Exactly the same happened to me, that's why..." I tried to explain, but he kept on as though he were completely oblivious to my presence.

"...began to do exercises. My body developed tremendously. One day my girlfriend pointed to a statue of the mythological god Atlas on a hotel roof and said to me: Look, you are just like that statue."

"Listen," I put in, "that statue..." It was no use. His voice swept on like a muddy river, brushing aside everything in its path.

"I stared up at the statue and thought to myself: you're not going to get ahead with a name like yours, people here are too prejudiced. Why not call yourself Atlas? And I also changed Angelino for Charles. Then came my days of glory. I can remember when I pulled a railcar full of chorus girls for two hundred yards..."

"Good God," I cried out, "exactly the same as..." but his voice, precise and eternal, ploughed on.

"Have you seen the statue of Alexander Hamilton outside the Treasury building in Washington? Well, that's me." He again raised his arms and made as though he were hauling a heavy weight, a railcar full of chorus girls perhaps. This time the pain must have been even more intense, because he groaned at length and fell prone on the bed. After a long while, he started to speak again, but by now all I wanted to do was leave.

"I remember Calabria," he said, squirming in the bed. The nurse tried to calm him, then went over to the trolley to make up some drops for him. "...Calabria, and my mother singing, her face ruddy from the flames of the oven." He gurgled something I couldn't follow, the sound of his voice echoing through the room in a series of agonised croaks. "A song..."

I had lost all notion of what was going on, when suddenly the insistent buzzing of a bell brought me back to myself. It resounded all down the corridors before bouncing back to its point of departure in the room, and I finally realized it came from the nurse tugging at a bell cord above the bed, while Charles Atlas lay sprawled naked on his back on the floor, spattered with blood, the metal plate dangling from his jaw.

All at once the room was filled with footsteps, voices, and shadows. I felt myself being lifted bodily from the chair by the same strong arms that had guided me there. In the jumble of images and sounds as I was being dragged from the room I heard the nurse cry out: "My God, the strain was too much for him; he couldn't resist that last pose!" and saw several men lifting the body onto a stretcher and hurrying it out.

Now, in old age as I write these lines, I still find it hard to believe that Charles Atlas isn't alive. I wouldn't have the heart to disillusion all the youngsters who write to him every day asking about his course, still under the spell of his colossal figure, his smiling, confident face, as he holds a trophy or hauls a railcar full of chorus girls, a hundred laughing, crushed girls waving their flowery bonnets through the windows, and in the incredulous crowds thronging the pavements to watch, a hand raises a hat to the sky.

I left New York the same night. I was weighed down with sorrow and remorse, convinced I was guilty in some way, if only of having witnessed such a tragedy. Back in Nicaragua, with Captain Hatfield USMC dead and the war over, I tried my hand at various things: working in a circus, as a weightlifter, then as a bodyguard. My physique isn't what it once was. Thanks to the Dynamic Tension System, though, I could still have children. If I wanted to.

1970

The Centerfielder

The flashlight picked out one prisoner after another until it came to rest on a bed where a man was asleep, his back to the door. His bare torso glistened with sweat.

"That's him, open up," said the guard, peering through the bars.

The warder's key hung from a length of electric cable he used as a belt. It grated in the rusty lock. Inside, the guards beat their rifle butts on the bedframe until the man struggled to his feet, shielding his eyes from the glare.

"Get up, you're wanted."

He was shivering with cold as he groped for his shirt, even though the heat had been unbearable all night, and the prisoners were sleeping in their underpants or stark naked. The only slit in the wall was so high up that the air never circulated much below the ceiling. He found his shirt, and poked his feet into his laceless shoes.

"Get a move on!" the guard said.

"I'm coming, can't you see?"

"Don't get smart with me, or else…"

"Or else what?"

"You know what else!"

The guard stood to one side to let him out of the cell. "Walk, don't talk," he snapped, jabbing him in the ribs with the rifle. The man flinched at the cold metal.

They emerged into the yard. Down by the far wall, the leaves of almond trees glittered in the moonlight. It was midnight, and the slaughtering of animals had begun in the next-door abattoir. The breeze carried a smell of blood and dung.

What a perfect field for baseball! The prisoners must make up teams to play, or take on the off-duty guards. The dugout would be the wall, which left about three hundred and fifty feet from home plate to centerfield. You'd have to field a hit from there running backwards toward the almond trees. When you picked up the ball the diamond would seem far away; the shouts for you to throw would be muffled by the distance; the batter would be rounding second base—and then I'd reach up, catch a branch, and swing myself up. I'd stretch forward, put my hands carefully between the broken bottles on the top of the wall, then edge over with my feet. I'd jump down, ignoring the pain as I crashed into the heap of garbage, bones, bits of horn, broken chairs, tin cans, rags, newspapers, dead vermin. Then I'd run on, tearing myself on thistles, stumbling into a drain of filthy water, but running on and on, as the dry crack of rifles sounded far behind me.

"Halt! Where d'you think you're going?"

"To piss, that's all."

"Scared are you?"

It is almost identical to the square back home, with the rubber trees growing right by the church steps. I was the only one on our team who had a real leather glove: all the others had to catch barehanded. I'd be out there fielding at six in the evening when it was so dark I could hardly see the ball. I could catch them like doves in my hand, just by the sound.

"Here he is, Captain," the guard called, poking his head around a half-open door. From inside came the steady hum of air conditioning.

"Bring him in, then leave us."

He felt immediately trapped in this bare, whitewashed room. Apart from a chair in the center, and the captain's desk up against the far wall, the only adornments were a gilt-framed portrait and a calendar with red and blue numbers. To judge by the fresh plaster, the air conditioning had only recently been installed.

"What time were you picked up?" the captain asked, without looking up.

He stood there at a loss for a reply, wishing with all his heart that the question had been aimed at somebody else—perhaps at someone hiding under the table.

"Are you deaf—I'm talking to you. What time were you taken prisoner?"

"Sometime after six, I reckon," he mumbled, so softly he was convinced the captain hadn't heard him.

"Why do you think it was after six? Can't you tell me the exact time?"

"I don't have a watch, sir, but I'd already eaten, and I always eat at six."

Come and eat, Ma would shout from the sidewalk outside the house. Just one more inning, I'd say, then I'll be there. But son, it's dark already, how can you see to play? I'm coming, there's only one inning left. The violin and the harmonium would be tuning up for Mass in the church as the ball flew safely into my hands for the last out. We'd won yet again.

"What job do you do?"

"I'm a cobbler."

"Do you work in a shop?"

"No, I do repairs at home."

"You used to be a baseball player, didn't you?"

"Yes, once upon a time."

"And you were known as 'Whiplash' Parrales, weren't you?"

"Yes, they called me that because of the way I threw the ball in."

"And you were in the national team that went to Cuba?"

"That's right, twenty years ago. I went as center-fielder."

"But they kicked you out..."

"When we got back."

"You made quite a name for yourself with that arm of yours." The captain's angry stare soon dashed the smile from Parrales' lips.

The best piece of fielding I ever did was at home when I caught a fly ball on the steps of the church itself. I took it with my back to the bases, but fell sprawling on my face and split my tongue. Still, we won the game and the team carried me home in triumph. My mother left her tortilla dough and came to care for my wound. She was sorry and proud at the same time: "Do you have to knock your brains out to prove you're a real sport?"

"Why did they kick you off the team?"

"On account of my dropping a fly and us losing the game."

"In Cuba?"

"We were playing Aruba. I bungled it, they got two runs, and we'd lost."

"Several of you were booted out, weren't you?"

"The fact is, we all drank a lot, and you can't do that in baseball."

"Aha!"

He wanted to ask if he could sit down because his shins were aching so, but didn't dare move an inch. Instead he stood stock still, as though his shoes were glued to the floor.

The captain laboriously wrote out something. He finally lifted his head, and Parrales could see the red imprint of a cap across his forehead.

"Why did they bring you in?"

He shrugged and stared at him blankly.

"Well, why?"

"No," he answered.

"No, what?"

"No, I don't know."

"Aha, so you don't know."

"No."

"I've got your file here," the captain said, flourishing a folder. Shall I read you a few bits so you can learn about yourself?" He stood up.

From centerfield you can barely hear the ball smack the catcher's mitt. But when the batter connects, the sound travels clearly and all your senses sharpen to follow the ball. As it flies through the distance to my loving hands, I wait patiently, dancing beneath it until finally I clasp it as though I'm making a nest for it.

"At five p.m. on July 28th a green canvas-topped jeep drew up outside your house. Two men got out: one was dark, wore khaki trousers, and sun glasses. The other was fair-skinned, wore bluejeans and a straw hat. The one with dark glasses was carrying a PanAm dufflebag; the other had an army backpack. They went into your house, and didn't come out again until ten o'clock. They didn't have their bags with them.''

''The one with the glasses...,'' nervous, he choked on endless saliva, ''he was my son, the one in glasses.''

''I know that.''

Again there was silence. Parrales' feet were perspiring inside his shoes, making them as wet as if he had just crossed a stream.

''The bag contained ammunition for a fixed machine gun, and the rucksack was full of fuses. When had you last seen your son before that?''

''Not for months,'' he murmured.

''Speak up, I can't hear you.''

''Months—I don't remember how many, but several months. He quit his job at the ropeworks one day, and we didn't see him again after that.''

''Weren't you worried about him?''

''Of course—he's my son, after all. We asked, made official enquiries, but got nowhere.'' Parrales pushed his false teeth back into place, worried in case the plate worked loose.

''Did you know he was in the mountains with the rebels?''

''We did hear rumors.''

''So when he turned up in the jeep, what did you think?''

''That he was coming home. But all he did was say hello, then leave again a few hours later.''

''And ask you to look after his things?''

''Yes, he said he'd send for them.''

''Oh, he did, did he?''

The captain pulled more purple-typed sheets out of the folder. He sifted through them, then laid one out on the desk.

"It says here that for three months you were handling ammunition, firearms, fuses and subversive literature, and that you let enemies of the government sleep in your house."

Parrales said nothing. He took out a handkerchief to blow his nose. He looked gaunt and shrunken in the lamplight, as though already reduced to a skeleton.

"And you weren't aware of a thing, were you?"

"You know what sons are."

"Sons of bitches, you mean."

Parrales stared down at the protruding tongues and the mud caking his tattered shoes.

"How long is it since you last saw your son?"

He looked the captain full in the face. "You know he's been killed, so why ask me that?"

The last inning of the game against Aruba, zero to zero, two outs, and the white ball was floating gently home to my hands as I waited, arms outstretched; we were about to meet for ever when the ball clipped the back of my hand, I tried to scoop it up, but it bounced to the ground—far off I could see the batter sliding home, and all was lost. Ma, I needed warm water on my wounds, like you always knew, I was always brave out on the field, even ready to die.

"Sometimes I'd like to be kind, but it's impossible," the captain said, advancing around the desk. He tossed the folder back into the drawer, and turned to switch off the air conditioning. Again the room was plunged into silence. He pulled a towel from a hook and draped it about his shoulders.

"Sergeant!" he shouted.

The sergeant stood to attention in the doorway. He led the prisoner out, then reappeared almost immediately.

"What am I to put in the report?"

"He was a baseball player, so make up anything you like. Say he was playing with the other prisoners, that he was centerfielder and chased a hit down to the wall, then climbed up an almond tree and jumped over the wall. Put down that we shot him as he was escaping across the slaughterhouse yard."

1967

The Siege

It was dusk when Septimio woke, and the rays of the setting sun were sparkling in the depths of the chiffonier's oval mirror like precious embers. The pages of a fashion magazine were stuck to his stomach with sweat. Naked beneath his silk kimono, he could feel the perspiration trickling down between his shoulder blades. As he stood up, he stumbled over the china tureen he had left on the floor. It shattered, and cold soup splashed his feet.

"Avelino," he whispered surreptitiously. "Avelino!" he called a second time, looking around for him in the gloom that neither of them could get accustomed to. They were always blundering into flower vases and chairs. They knocked over the plaster statues, then had to grope to replace them on their tables, or push the pieces against the skirting until they could sweep them up along with all the rubbish thrown at them, by the feeble glow of the altar light in the bedroom or the angel's torch if they had lit it.

"Avelino," he called out once more, his voice by now almost a whimper. Night was falling rapidly outside; the six o'clock train whistled in the distance.

They must be coming by now, if they hadn't already surrounded the house, crawling their way through the coffee bushes and snipping the wire fences. They would be hidden behind the tree trunks or would be up in the branches, silently, ruthlessly demolishing the garden.

"Open the door," he heard.

"Who is it?" he asked.

"It's me—quick."

"Is that you, Avelino?"

Septimio crawled over to the door. Outside, the stairs ended in a small landing. He was nerving himself to turn the white egg of the doorknob, slippery from his moist palm, when he caught the sound of stifled laughter on the other side.

"Who's there?" he shouted in terror.

"It's me, Avelino, open up."

"Is that really you, Avelino?"

"Yes of course, dearie," came the sniggering reply.

"Go to hell," he screamed, though he was unsure whether his words were audible or merely came out as a choked sob.

Bewildered, he retreated to the living room and propped himself against his mother's piano, where a family of mice was nesting. The previous night's siege had left him and Avelino broken in spirit and in body after they had put out the blaze in the kitchen, and then had to abandon the orchard to their attackers. They had ducked under the four-poster bed and sheltered there until daybreak from the stones that rained in through the shattered windows. At first light they had crept out bleary-eyed through the glass door to the balcony and wearily began to sweep up all the stones and unripe fruit that littered the parquet floor. The mist had lifted and the palm trees were swaying in the morning breeze. From the balcony they could see the railway siding, where a handful of men trudged along the tracks to work.

He was still cowering by the piano when the walls of the house started to shake to an unbearable rhythm. Then stones began to land on the roof tiles, which broke and crashed down onto the ceiling above him. Outside, people were tearing at the branches of the fruit trees, uprooting the fences. He crawled through the doorway and locked himself in the bedroom.

"Too bad for Avelino," he whined. "Nobody told him to go out." Now, for the first time he had to face the attacks alone, and suddenly as he edged under the bed for shelter he was hit by the smell of stale urine, spit, and foul shoes from the floor. The rough boards scratched at the flaccid skin of his naked torso, and the medallion he always wore around his neck jabbed into him. Apart from the house and grounds, it was all he had inherited from his mother, a lock of whose hair he kept in it. Avelino's only legacy from his mother had been the angel.

They had been forced to abandon the ground floor, which they had previously used to store coffee beans and gardening tools. Once Avelino had gone down there barefoot to the bathroom beyond the kitchen; he had found the hand-basin full of dead mice floating among the magnolia and jasmine petals they put in the water every afternoon to perfume it. Disgusted, Avelino picked them up one by one by their tails and threw them out into the yard. He spent the whole morning being sick, and refused to eat lunch. It was then they decided never again to venture down to the bathroom or toilet, and instead on relied on the rose-patterned chamber pots they kept in the bedroom.

He heard stones pattering on the roof again. This time

they sounded like an endless rainstorm, and he couldn't help wondering where Avelino was: what can they be doing to you all alone out there in the dark, poor captive Avelino? The stones thundered down like the day of the last judgement.

In one corner of the room stood the angel Avelino had inherited. It was a life-sized plaster figure, with real herons' feathers for wings. Once a month they removed the purple tunic with its gold embroidery to clean it, and then the angel was left completely naked. Before they became victims of the siege, they would light the angel's torch as they went to bed, and lie there in its flickering light making believe they had been locked in a church somewhere.

Now he could make out clearly the sound of footsteps on the roof, and plaster from the ceiling mouldings showered the furniture. He hid his head in his hands, as if the pieces could hit him even under the bed. Suddenly, an image of his mother came into his mind.

"It hurts here," she had said, pointing to her chest as she was feeding bananas to the green parrots in their cages, and then slid to the ground and lay in a heap next to the sink. Her tiny purple mouth kissed the air as though she were thanking the audience at the end of one of her operatic recitals, but her face was pallid, with none of the paint she used to wear to make herself look rosy-cheeked in the footlights (the same she used to retouch her saints' faces) but which made her cheeks so taut she could never smile to acknowledge the applause. She lay there, tiny and fragile in her green velvet dress, a paper rose at the neck, on her feet the suede slippers battered out of shape by sun and rain. He had run over from pruning the rose bushes and knelt beside her as she breathed her last, on that golden afternoon, miles from the nearest town.

So he was left in charge of the garden, with its *araucarias,* hedgerows, and the cypresses beyond the house that made the far side as gloomy as a cemetery. He had to look after the cages, an ant-eaten dovecote high in a *chilamate* tree, rose bushes and begonias, and the two-story house as well, its balconies floating in the dawn mists. And he was all alone to tend the coffee plantation shaded by banana trees, and the orchard full of oranges, limes, medlars, sweet lemons and guavas. Until one day Avelino, who had also lost his mother, arrived from another village. Septimio took him in, and from that moment the two lived in the house together, getting by on what they could sell of flowers and fruit. A week after Avelino moved in, his angel was brought to the station by train, then carted up to the house.

"Couldn't we give it to the church?" Septimio had suggested when he saw how big it was. But Avelino got so upset, because it was all he had to remember his mother by, that Septimio hadn't insisted.

"You'll destroy the house," he shouted from under the bed. By now they were scampering all over the roof. "Come down from there, dammit," he shrieked, but this only made things worse, and tiles began to cascade down into the yard. He guessed they must want to get in via the roof. Then they would rip up the boards on the ceiling. And all they had to do to reach the balcony was to sling ropes around the pillars then swarm up. Or they could jump down out of the trees onto the landing; the glass door was only bolted, and if they smashed the glass they could easily get in. Perhaps they didn't know that.

Fewer tiles seemed to be crashing down now.

"Get off there, will you?" he begged them.

"This isn't something I like doing, but it's my duty," the inspector had said. "We've received complaints that you two are cohabiting immorally."

"Who says so?" Septimio had asked, deeply offended.

"It doesn't matter who, but word has it that you two have set up house together, that you never leave the place, that you don't behave like men. I'm only here to warn you. I won't have any indecency in this town, so be careful."

"Captain," Septimio put in, "you know it's only malicious gossip…"

"That may be: how on earth should I know? But just watch how you behave. Why don't you act your age, Septimio, you're old enough to be my father."

A crowd was waiting for them as they left the police station, and a gang of children ran after them to the edge of the village, shouting abuse. That was the night the siege began.

Septimio had no idea what time it might be; he had a bitter taste in his mouth and a terrible thirst. He couldn't remember how long he'd been in that same position. It must have been hours. The noises on the roof ceased and he could hear voices fading in the distance. That's the way it always is, you think they're leaving then all of a sudden they come back again. What can they have done to Avelino? He's not as strong as he looks; he can't take much because of his asthma. He dozed off with the stench from the floor in his nostrils, watched over by all the angels of the house. He had only come to love them once Avelino's life-sized heavyweight had been coaxed into the bedroom to take its place alongside the heavenly hosts his mother had strewn everywhere. Cherubim topped the bedposts; two angels entwined in a passionate embrace round the frame of the huge mirror in the living room; entire armies of angels riding their clouds careered across wardrobe doors and the walls.

He could hear the voices near the house again. He knew what they were doing: they were relieving themselves in the begonias—the rivulets streamed across the garden. He thought of Avelino defenceless out there in the hands of those brutes who were pissing in the flower tubs; Avelino, delicate as a flower; taking turns to piss, Avelino. He was only half-awake; his hands were numb and covered in saliva from gagging himself with them in an attempt to choke back the suffering. Suddenly he heard Avelino's voice calling him. He hadn't the faintest idea how much later this was.

"It's me, Avelino—open up." The sound only just reached him from somewhere down on the ground.

"Who's that out there?" he asked.

"It's me, open the door."

"Is this another trick?"

"No. Open the door so I can come up."

Septimio crawled over to the glass door and cautiously pushed it open. He saw day was dawning.

"Avelino, where are you?"

"I'm down here in the garden, can't you see me?"

Septimio got to his knees and peered over the balustrade.

"Open up, for God's sake."

"Have they gone?"

"Yes, they're far away by now."

Scarcely able to stand, Septimio crossed the bedroom, staggered through the living room, and opened the door at the top of the stairs. Avelino stood there exhausted, his forehead streaming blood, his body lost inside a huge pair of trousers. Septimio led him over to the rocking chair to examine at the wound over his eyebrow.

"What made you go out?"

"I was hungry and went to get something to eat."

"You went into town?"

"I ran into them on the way back. They dragged me here."

Septimio settled him gently into the chair, then went to fetch some alcohol from a drawer in the chiffonier. He also brought a sheet, which he tore into strips to make a bandage, and a washbowl.

"You shouldn't have gone out, Avelino."

"I was starving, and I thought I'd be back before nightfall."

Septimio wiped his bloodstained face.

"Are you sure they won't return?"

"No, not now. They pissed on the flowers; they let me go, then they left."

"Sit still, you've got a bad cut. Sometimes when you think they've gone for good, they sneak back."

"No, not this time, it's already daylight."

Septimio moved the bowl away from the rocking chair, and folded up the piece of the sheet he didn't need. He put on his glasses to inspect the wound before bandaging it.

"Does it hurt?"

"Like hell."

"What did they do to you?" he asked as he wrapped the cloth around.

"Nothing. They just tried to scare me."

Septimio didn't say a word. Avelino fumbled with the buttons of his shirt, and his paunch flopped over the waistband of his trousers.

"They threw stones at me," he sobbed. His gold teeth glinted.

"D'you see why you ought never to go out?"

"But I was really hungry. I bought some crackers and a tin of sardines."

Septimio finished the bandage, then steered Avelino into the bedroom and helped him lie on the bed. Avelino touched his wound, and called out: "Septimio!"

"What is it?"

"They took me off into the bushes."

The angel stood naked in its corner.

"Tomorrow we must remember to dress the angel," Septimio said, stretching out beside him.

"Yes, tomorrow." Avelino's head was throbbing so much he kept his eyes closed tight as he spoke. "They told me: keep your mouth shut or we'll do you in."

"What are they like, Avelino?"

"Filthy, cruel," he answered softly.

Mist swirled into the room. In the bed, Septimio was almost bald; it looked as though someone had anointed Avelino's head with ashes.

1967

A Bed of Bauxite in Weipa

The plane again.

"It'll take at least an hour and a half along that narrow road with the drop on one side," said Harry, "and at every curve you think the car's going to fly off into some roadside saloon."

"Let's drink to the well-being of our souls." Walter raised his glass. "Spending a few days shut away doesn't worry me. My wife's given herself a holiday too."

The plane passed over once more through the darkening sky, its engines like an angel making music with the wind and rain, the noise swelling and fading like the harmonies of a distant choir. He lay there, staring at the ceiling, waiting for the plane's next sweep. But now there were peals of thunder and rain started to pour. He could hear it lashing against the windows behind the drawn curtains, flooding from the window boxes down onto the tiles, streaming out to the drains. Gradually the rain settled to a steady drumming, a concert of sounds beyond his room, a leaden curtain that enveloped streets and trees, shutting out the horizon, the cypress-lined avenues, the hills and the ravines, where the streams gushed swollen with dirty flood water. The plane circled overhead again, but this time he was barely able to make out its ululating music as it drifted down out of the sullen sky, all quicksilver, lashing fury, then a gentle dampness, an age-old silence, an unassailable serenity. He had woken, curled in the warmth of the grey woollen blanket and white sheets, to the feeling of intimacy that rain brings deep inside. The wind rattled the doors in his dark kingdom of silence. The house was immersed in this weighty gloom, with armchairs, paintings, tables all submerged in it as though stranded for ever in an immutable, untouchable order. His kingdom. The cars on the highway sent sheets of spray high into the air, honking their horns in the mist.

His own gaunt features appeared as though in a blurred snapshot behind his wife's ritual objects in the large dressing table mirror.

"We're getting on, Oreamuno."

"Yes, gorgeous, we're getting on."

"You'll look after him for me, won't you, Harry?"

"I'll keep him busy with the courses, Julie. He's not going to wriggle out of it this time."

"I don't want to hear any stories when I get back. I have my spies, you know."

"I promise there'll be nothing to complain about," said Walter, suddenly serious.

"Who knows," said Julie with a smile. "We'll see."

The clock by the bed showed five twenty. His mind plotted the sequence of actions that would follow his getting up. First he'd put on the slippers and the red silk bathrobe folded over the chair he liked to read in, under the fringed lampshade. Next he'd give his early morning face the once over in the mirror of the bathroom cabinet, open it for the Listerine mouthwash, slip off the dressing gown on to the marble bench (the donning of the priestly

robe is for a few brief moments only), then finally completely naked he'd settle on the beige-colored porcelain bowl
to read the book he always left on the top of the lavatory,
right next to the toilet roll, neatly disguised under its knit-
ted cover. This was his morning book, as sacred to this hour
as a prayer book, not to be touched by other hands or at
other hours of the day.

"Hey, Harry, you're sure they ask no questions?"

"Nah, you can trust the priest. Nobody who goes there
has a past. You're your own conscience, you talk only if
the spirit moves you. If not, you don't have to say a word,
they leave you in peace."

"You can imagine what a jerk I'd feel confessing in
public."

"I'm telling you: nobody is forcing you."

He pulled back the pink curtain with its pattern of
snow-white swans and turned on the tap to test the water.
The chorus of the plane's engine rang out again overhead:

> In colors
> In colors are clothed
> all the fields in the spring...

Marylin, your scent of pencils, chalk, shavings from
sharpeners, school desks, all the unidentifiable odors of the
playground, a slow, soft basketball and you in gym slip,
of sweat plastering the hair to your forehead, of the deep
pockets in your blue-striped uniform, the smell of your
snacks of mangoes, guavas and almonds, of your warm
white skin under the black cotton stockings, stiff petticoats,
of vaseline in your pony-tailed hair, of a light shimmering
in the dark, of a red tip at the foot of a statue in the chapel

of mystery heaped with flowers and vases, of your seclus-ion, of dormitory and prefect's room, of prize-day plays, with you dressed up as an angel with tinsel wings, behind you a timid choir and unobtrusive piano, of end-of-term reports, Marylin, studious, excellent, respectful, good con-duct, blue ribbon, daughter of Mary, communicant, apostolic mission, postulant, of the community's untouchable order, of afternoon teas and cakes, of veil and best uniform, and of English/Hamilton, French/Godard, Grammar/Bruno, of instruments, of inkwells, of 24-page lined writing tablets, dividers and a clean book, of sew-ing, stitching, and embroidery, of a habit stiff with sweat, of Gregorian chant, of novitiate Mass, of bells for lunch and dinner, now here I see you Marylin before Mother Superior the fifth year wish to offer you this token of their appreciation on your birthday, dear Mother, she touches your blushing cheek, thank you my precious, of communal showers clinging to the chain, the water moulding the nightdress to your body, of 8 sheets, 4 pillow-cases, 6 uniforms, one best uniform, 12 pairs ankle socks, 2 pairs shoes, 6 pairs bloomers, 6 brassieres, 2 veils, of a furtive letter tossed in through the dormitory window and opened during prep, of let's all sing Love Divine All Loves Excell-ing, of God in Heaven and Here on Earth, of candelabra, of choir, of altar cloth, of the organ, of monstrance, of lilies of the valley, of endless stone corridors you walked along in your sleep, of barred windows you make signals through, of the tiled yard where you fell and scraped your knees so badly they bled, of that archway you disappeared through like a prisoner, of the blossoming innocence of your body— all this is your perfume, Marylin, mingling tonight with the scent of your tousled hair and lipstick as you languidly undress in my arms.

"Say when."

"Not too much for me, *licenciado*. It's too early to drink."

He unscrewed the top and placed two tumblers on the glass table. He poured whiskey on the rocks.

"Are you sure two weeks will be enough? That's how long I'll be in Dallas."

"Trust me. By the time you're back, the permit will be on your desk."

"It's just that it's taken such an age—it's been six months already."

"You know how tricky all this official business is, they're so touchy about these concessions involving national pride."

The American burst out laughing, then spluttered. He was bull-necked, with a crewcut. He wore enormous clown's shoes and a bile-coloured tie. He stood up and leaned over the metal desk.

"Mister Thomas, would it bother you if I sent your office a small bill?"

"Oh?" Thomas smiled, unenthusiastically.

"Nothing much—a few expenses. My wife's vacation. And you know, sometimes it's not easy, people won't play ball, and that holds everything up."

Thomas' laugh again ended in a coughing fit.

"When does your wife get back?"

"In another week, more or less."

"Say hello to her from me, *licenciado*."

He opened the door, then closed it quietly behind his departing visitor. The din from the snarled-up traffic down in the street came and went. He yawned and shifted in his seat, then pressed the intercom. In a few seconds his secretary would be standing tall and cool in the doorway, dousing his senses with her fragrance of eau de Cologne.

Such a cruel night, Marylin, our eyes desolate in the Ukranian darkness full of calm stars, chilled by the wind sweeping down from the pale sky, *mujik*, andromeda—my hand caressing your swan's neck, a bed of snow and an ermine cover, together we crossed the terrors of the Tropic, scorched in Isabelia, set sail for Cayenne clinging to the mainmast tossed on the stormy blue sea, dozed on the coral reefs, then you the lofty one, the seer, you the harpy, the dagger, the hermit crab, warming grebe and heron chicks in the palm of your hand, your warm breath on their fragile heads, then us making love on a bed of bauxite in Weipa by the side of the polished, precious Timor Sea, in Sydney walking hand-in-hand through a square full of purple and ash-grey pigeons to the cries of the wool-dealers thronging the salesroom in the Royal Exchange, while from the fluffy sky a fine fleece of rain came down, your pale blue eyes darting to and fro over the death of Sardanapalus, stroking the canvas of Saint André in Morreau, our stealthy meeting among the loving couples in the flag-yard of Robert College, Istanbul, the fierce cutting sandstorm in the Libyan desert, then Maisa Brega, huddled against the wall that shields saplings from the wind, trees planted to help stabilise the dunes, a moist, unmoving hand on mine, your hand on mine, tapping in a gentle rhythm while the freezing wind from the Wannsee stings our faces even though it's summertime in Berlin, should we risk a boat? Then Tripoli,

Marbella, Lake Invernada in the Chilean Andes, strolling at dusk across the bridge on the river Krk, you gazing up at the flying buttresses, me at the unique redeeming flamboyant ogive, the wretched drawn-out farewell in the bungalow at the Game Lodge in Kenya, surrounded by the skins and heads of stuffed animals, since when and where I have never seen you again, free woman, prisoner, everlasting, iron maiden, vixen, it was a starry dream that fell to earth, the distant roar of the sea unfurling in the North African twilight, a hand pressed round the heart of a ring-tailed dove, probing the wound with your fingers, a caress of ashes, the vows we made, your head crowned with bougainvillea, you stained pink in the dying light, passionflowers, a handkerchief, a spent flashbulb, a leaf, ecstasy, mystery.

"Always with a glass in your hand."

"That's the life."

"When does your wife get back?"

"Today."

"You don't say."

"Uhuh."

"Farewell, sweet bachelor life then."

"You got it."

"But you can't tell me those days in our retreat didn't do the trick. You're a changed man," Harry said slyly.

"What crap you talk," Walter replied, annoyed. He straightened his sunglasses as he spoke. They were having lunch, poolside at the club. Harry carried on eating in silence. The sky was cloudy, and there were only three people in the pool.

"If you didn't put your time near to God to good use,"

Harry chuckled, "you sure got something somewhere, didn't you?"

"What on earth are you talking about?"

"With God or with the Devil. The flesh, you old fucker."

"I'll accept the *old*."

"Brother, you're over the top. My wife and I went out for a drive the other night. When we passed your place, the hi-fi was going full blast, all the lights were on. Is Walter throwing a party? Louise asked me. He likes to drink alone, I told her. Then I pulled up on the other side of the avenue."

"So you spy on me these days?"

"What about that retreat you went on, Louise wanted to know, didn't it teach either of you anything? Don't generalize, honey, I told her. You men are all the same. So what's so terrible about Walter sitting up there having a drink? I bet you he's not on his own, she said—and you know how women can smell these things a mile off. They're unbelievable."

"What things?"

"The smell of female, the honey-dew..."

And in September Marylin there you were flitting like a startled deer among your classmates at the St. Brigide College in Baton Rouge. Autumn was turning the chestnut tree leaves as you stared at the dull red river waters, in the distance the blacks naked to the waist digging with their hoes, the grain silos as tall as church spires, half-listening to Miss Anthonie Cornellie trying to teach you English by reciting Marlowe, her bifocals dangling from a golden chain, her shrivelled lips chanting the verses, you couldn't understand a word of her warbling, but gazed out at the strange effortless birds gliding through the dusk sky while beside you a bunch of wildflowers wilted in a plaster vase on the mantelpiece in the tiny drawing-room where you suffered your lessons, sunk back in a faded chintz armchair. Miss Cornellie, slight and querulous, pacing from door to window, window to bookcase, the daughter of a second violinist in the Boston Pops, however much her reedy voice suggests descent from wild plantation owners of Louisiana, tamers of negroes and horses, she the spinster dead-end of the line, but you Marylin dreaming of your loved one who keeps you waiting beyond nightfall, the meadows with their cool smell of hay wafting in through the window, you turning your face to the Tropics while on the blackboard, the teacher lists the irregular English verbs, intoning their conjugation as though they were the secret formulae of a spell. You are dimly aware of the bell for tea in the bright, airy, glass-roofed dining room, saying goodbye to the teacher and slipping out to join your mates in the walk, while she stands there, piece of chalk still in her hand, halfway through the act of writing something, then the cup of tea, donuts and slices of lemon, speaking secretly in Spanish to each other when the lookout who patrols the tables to see only English is spoken goes out of earshot. You wrapped in the memory of the boy who is simply waiting for you to finish this bilingual education, flower arranging, good housekeeping, social graces, fashion and the correct use of make-up, St. Brigide like a dream, the airline ticket in the calfskin bag on the night table all set for the trip to the United States early the next morning. Once in New Orleans, you and your mother carefully chose at Maison Blanche all the clothes you might need: delicate blouses, high-class underwear, shoes and dresses for cocktail parties, slacks for your weekends with the boys and girls in their convertibles, the dances and the barbecues in public parks, records on the portable player. Then the day of your return, heralded in all the social columns of the newspapers, with a picture of you, a woman of marrying age now, with all the accomplishments, the same young man still waiting, dancing with you at all the welcome-home balls, the warmth of the hand he holds out to you is beyond compare. You're talking alone with him, you tell him all the crazy things like when the girls jumped fully clothed into the pool, or hid from the *gringos* who came to visit in their open-topped cars, and as you recount all your pranks, my back turned to the night, I count the golden strands of your hair, the tiny freckles on the nape of your neck.

"You know my lips are sealed," Harry said to him as they paid the bill.

"You'll laugh at me, you old son-of-a-bitch, but I really miss my wife," he said, hauling himself to his feet.

"The eternal creature of habit."

"Or of habits of creatures," he said, slapping Harry on the back.

"Don't forget now."

"Forget what?"

"The flowers. A basket of flowers in the drawing room is the best sweetener."

He smiled feebly. The sky was darkening over, and the chain of mountains around the city was disappearing behind banks of heavy cloud. Not a ripple disturbed the surface of the swimming pool. Nobody was in the stables or on the golf course, the waiters were having lunch. The car park was deserted.

"You may not believe this, but I can hardly wait for her to arrive."

Harry made no comment. The two of them walked along the corridor, whistling different tunes to themselves.

"I'm off to sleep a while," said Harry. "Saturday at last."

"I'll call you Monday."

"Okay. Don't forget the flowers, now," he reminded him as he started the car.

Nodding, he waved Harry good-bye. Red roses, he thought to himself. A bouquet on the sideboard.

You Marylin I'll welcome in the drawing room used for our special occasions, so wide and spacious, with no secret corners, its downy sofas, soft armchairs, wall-to-wall carpeting, abstract paintings, bronze statuettes, porcelain and Murano glass vases, unseen music coming from speakers concealed behind the diffused lights, you'll sit like a sovereign to listen to Bach soaring from the pipes of the silvery organs hidden in the shadows, played by ethereal fingers to lead us from dream to dream, you I'll allow to cross the threshold of this place of rituals, reserved for the most outstanding occasions, like the fifteenth birthday of Lucinda, who's at finishing school in Berne, Fred's end-of-school celebration before he went to study electromechanics at Loyola University, our wedding anniversaries when the two of us, bashful and blushing as the musicians installed on their improvised stage at the far end of the room struck up the anniversary waltz, began to dance to affectionate applause, only you may enter these sealed walls, this temple of offerings, this site of burnt incense, only you, Marylin, tall and chaste, proud and haughty, diaphanous and sure, you may stroll here in your kingdom, light the candles and turn off the lights, disrobe to wrap yourself in the endless wail of Charlie Rouse's saxophone, to your own rhythm, virgin in the bed of the pastor who is filling the glasses with Smirnoff, and in your name is opening the cans of tomato juice.

He signalled to the right. Light rain began to fall as he turned by the statue of León Cortés by the old airport at La Sabana. The ponies in the children's playground were tugging at their reins, anxious to find shelter. It was cold, so he zipped his jacket up to the neck. He turned on the windshield wipers; by the time he had pulled out on to the Cañas highway, the rain was coming down steadily. He switched on the radio: Khachaturian and static. The wipers steadily swept the streams of water from the glass. The cars on the far side of the road loomed dimly through the mist. Some of them had their headlights on. He glanced at the clock on the dashboard: too bad, my love. If the plane can't land, it'll mean another day without you. This damn rain day and night. You'll have to sleep in Panama. Nobody to make my breakfast or anything. The two ailing maids who looked after him went down with colds as soon as they smelled rain, and hadn't shown up in a week. So he'd been preparing his own breakfast, clumsily making his own coffee, rummaging in all the cupboards to find a cup, spoon, the instant coffee, the sugar bowl. That was all he'd had in his stomach this morning until lunchtime; he'd decided to add a shot of whiskey to the coffee though, and a warm glow spread through him. No sense in breaking the habit too abruptly. Then he called his secretary at the office and was told there were no clients to see him. Saturday. All of them would come rushing in on Monday with urgent business. For a while he had stood staring through the window at the rain, listening to music.

When the weather cleared, he decided to go out and pick Harry up at his office. The plane wasn't due to arrive until five, so they went for lunch. Anything was better than moping about under this lowering sky.

There's no place as bad as Puerto Cabezas in the rainstorms, when the streets turn to muddy fields. On Sunday mornings we had to leap the puddles on our way to service at the Moravian Church, set in a deserted square lined with bare oaks, clouds of mosquitos swarming around the wooden spire. The sea is warm and oily, full of coconut tree branches swept along by the currents together with kerosene cans, broken chairs, the sea a garbage dump, one day the spongy corpse of a drowned man floating beyond the bushes, a boat whose towrope the wind has snapped drifting from its moorings to the dismay of the shouting, wide-eyed fishermen, howling like banshees on the shoreline, hurricane at midnight clawing at the corrugated iron roofs, water flooding the land, up to the very top of the house stilts, dawn revealing the whole landscape flooded and filthy. I carried a slate and chalk, a child's spelling book, a canvas satchel and my umbrella, its mother-of-pearl handle worn smooth by the years, across the gullies to the

Moravian school where they taught me religion and how
to sing hymns in English. Míster Rupert the pastor was
the schoolteacher. When I was fifteen I came here to Puerto
Limón on a tugboat. I was always brought up among
blacks, in Puerto Cabezas, in Puerto Limón. In Puerto
Cabezas I had to take off my drunken father's shoes and
wash my rheumatic mother's back, rubbing her with
alcohol; here I set up house with a linesman from the
Northern Railway, waiting for him till midnight with his
foodbox, listening for the whistle of trains to San José, the
saddest sound in the whole world. Dancing in black men's
clubs, drinking, going to bed with them, me, the queer one,
the white girl, the stranger in their neighborhoods, with
their wooden verandas, their window boxes, tiled floors,
strings of laundry, the smell of tar and frying, mustiness
and toilets, kerosene, dirty washing and fleas, stagnant
water and the brothel bedrooms, walls decorated with
pictures of women saints, hearts pierced by golden dag-
gers, dank mattresses, chamber pots, tinfoil stuffed in the
cracks of the windows. One day when I was already on the
game there was a drunken brawl, the man at my table got
his face slashed with a bottle. I spent two months in jail;
there was no women's cell so I slept in the sheriff's office.
He gave me enough money to reach San José, and here
my luck has taken a turn for the better, *licenciado*.

Unexpectedly, by the time he reached the airport a hesitant
sun was peeping through the clouds. There was only a film
of moisture on the windshield, so he switched off the wipers.
He studied himself in the mirror, smoothed down his
thinning hair with his left hand. Time marches on, as he

slowed for the terminal, but you have to try to take care of yourself, it's nonsense that drink ages you, or having a good time, it's routine and boredom that make you old. Now studying his profile, no need to go out so often, make sure each time is a real occasion, and no more girls in the house. That morning, after his breakfast in the kitchen, he had come across a small plastic comb with a few strands of blond hair in it as he crossed the drawing room to open the curtains. He picked it up and held it to the light, then put it in his pocket. On the drive to the airport he threw it out of the car window. He'd also cleared away the glasses and taken them to the kitchen. He carefully wiped the lipstick from one of them, couldn't think what to do with the handkerchief, then finally stifled the red spot in the wash-basin as if it had been a hot ember. He lifted the bin-lid and dropped it in. Everything was as it should be, back to normal. No smell in the bedroom of alcohol or women. The early morning rain had washed away the smell of bodies. As he was leaving, the sight of his ageing features in the ornate framed mirror gave him a shock. He ducked his chin and sheepishly examined his scalp, with the repugnant tonsure spreading on his crown. Still standing by the mirror, he lit a cigarette, then flicked his wrist to extinguish the match. He walked over to the bronze ashtray and gently deposited it there. The sealed kingdom, peopled once again with stately gestures.

"The airplane is on time, sir."

The cement floors, chairs upturned on tables, when all of us girls were given breakfast, the jukebox in its shroud, red and green lights turned off, spiders crawling over the bulbs, on the bandstand the instruments lying in silence, the music stands like the skeletons of household pets, hens scratching in between the tables, the barman cleaning the glasses monotonously, whistling to himself, my clothes in the maroon wardrobe with its print of Our Lady of the Angels next to a picture of Pedro Infante torn from a music sheet and others of unrecognisable singers, the dresses hanging in their row by my bed, the window looking out on a yard littered with beer crates and bits of junk, provocative dresses of taffeta and tulle, sequins and gaudy corsets for our flesh in its inevitable decline to a nameless old age, arriving at the beach without estuary lit by a dull, sepulchral moon, my arrival at the end, the very end and will there be God or not, against the wall your votive lamp, if not Him then who, dear mother, swindler, filthy beast, drunkard, you're insatiable, pastor Rupert, the first and the foulest, we're fine deep down in our soul, honeydew, a child deep inside headless can you imagine that, lonely owl whenever an abortion is needed or a wire, like a picklock, headfirst out into the world, the multicolored calendar, colors of the light, colors of the music, solitary star, the light extinguished, the day full only of shadows, this far and no further here we have reached here we will stay I set out on this path alone with grieving soul as the lengthy shadows stretched from the roadside trees, I asked if they could hear me but nobody, only this voice, one voice, this is your destiny, so on I went, wake up Marylin you fell asleep, come on up you get, no need to shout *licenciado* I'm not deaf, if you like it that's fine, if not that's fine too, is it raining in the port, *licenciado*, or is it only the sea?

"Just as I was saying."

"What exactly were you saying?" asked Walter.

"That you're a hoot with the whores."

"Why?"

"All that stuff you ask them like how did you get into this, haven't you got a family, what about your mother?"

"You're making it up," he grunted.

"I've heard you with my own ears."

"Well, even if it's true, aren't they people just like us? They have their feelings too."

"Their heart of gold."

"There must be some reason for them to fall so low."

"Can't you see how ridiculous you are? First you use them, then you feel sorry for them. You're one of the sort who say, forgive me, Lord, for the evil I'm about to commit."

"I think you're missing the point, Harry."

"I'll tell you what I think—that in spite of everything, those talks on Christianity scored a hit with you. Didn't I tell you you look a changed man, your face is different, like you've got an inner light. Even more than Father Ferrán."

"You're crazy, I swear. It was you who dragged me to that place, you skunk. But you'll never get me back there, I promise you."

"Yes, friend, you'll be back; every sin needs its remission, its instantaneous punishment, a penance here on earth. Up there the priests and everyone else gave you absolution in our midst; we all absolved each other. So now you're pure again to see whether you're strong enough to confront sin, while the world goes on turning."

"You sound just like a Bible broadcast."

"I'm telling you, you'll go back. We all like it."

"Like what, precisely?"

"To confuse the desire with the intention. Now I'm off," he said, rising to his feet and walking off, chuckling to himself.

"You learned more than me," Walter called out, "you're already preaching."

"That's because I'm a regular," Harry called over his shoulder, "a real believer."

"So you're black?" he asked.

"With a white soul though," the girl laughed.

"What about your skin? And you've got blonde hair."

"There's nature for you, *licenciado*. I've been told that if I have a kid, it'll be black as soot."

"Marylin, that deserves a drink." He stood up and went over to the built-in bar cabinet, its doors lined with mirrors.

"Tell me again about the college in the United States, *licenciado*. I love hearing that one."

He smiled, and went on pouring the drinks.

"Come on, tell me."

"Some other time."

"We girls always had stories we made up, or heard other people telling, or read in books. They always start: I used to be a respectable woman in good society. It was bad luck that brought me this low; I had a good education, everybody loved me...Why aren't you drinking?"

"I'm listening."

"My father is always writing telling me to get out, to go to Europe on a trip, but I've never accepted. You look very grand like that, frank and decent, like with your clients, *licenciado*."

"What are you saying now?"

"There used to be a young girl with us. She had a lovely body, pale blue eyes, hair down to her waist, a real beauty. She always got more money by bursting into tears just as they were about to pay her, sobbing out her misfortune, how she had found her husband with another woman, so she was doing this out of revenge."

"Now we really have to get drunk, you've upset me."

"How?"

"That story about the blacks." He stood up and pulled back the curtain. A red glow suffused the dark sky, like a distant bonfire.

"Put on that record I like."

"Strangers in the Night?"

"Yeah, that's it."

He vanished for a moment behind the carved oak door, then the music began to well up from hidden speakers. Marylin picked her dress from the floor and stepped into her shoes as she did the zipper up her back.

"Is Marylin your real name?"

"No, I just use it for work," she said, a hairpin between her teeth. The phone rang. He picked it up distractedly, as if it were a bird's fluttering wing. He spoke distantly, as though to some other country, some other dream, some other evening, some other twilight. By the time he had finished, she was standing in the doorway, swinging her cheap plastic bag from her shoulder.

"Where are you going?"

"Home. I feel sad."

In a short while he heard a growing rumble and, leaning on the terrace balcony, he watched as the Trident landed, taxied across the tarmac, then stopped by the steps, its tiny blue lights winking high on the tail and wings.

She was last off the plane, slender and lithe as she waved a white-gloved hand to him, shaking the charms on her bracelet. She waved again as she crossed to the terminal, and he blew her a kiss. The he trod out his cigarette.

"I've missed you so much, darling."

"You too, Oreamuno, if only you knew..."

He kissed the corner of her mouth. Her skin tasted of cosmetics.

"Any news?"

"None."

"Been behaving yourself?"

"Need you ask?"

"What about that religious retreat?"

"Ah yes, crazy Harry's famous courses."

"I've brought you records, and ties."

Night was falling as he pulled out onto the highway. His face, when he checked again in the mirror, was the same as ever.

1968

Nicaragua is White

The book by Brückner must be around somewhere, buried perhaps under the piles of old weather reports that had been accumulating ever since the Observatory had been founded, lost among the mounds of pink sheets typed on the same Remington and then telegraphed each day to villages throughout the country for distribution to local farmers before nightfall. The messengers rode from ranch to ranch, through sugar fields and coffee plantations, to deliver the forecasts of wind and rain: unless that is, they never bothered to deliver them at all, but simply made paper boats of the bulletins and sailed them off down the rivers, or threw them onto their fires once the mailbags slung across their horses' flanks were crammed to overflowing.

The Cyclical Theory by Brückner was the only one that contained the scale of wind speeds perfected by Beaufort in 1869. Once he could check that they were equivalent to 0.12 on that scale, the calculations he had been busy with since dawn would be complete. He hadn't bothered to draw up the usual daily weather report: it was December, everybody knew it wasn't going to rain, and that the temperature would still be dropping at sea level on the Pacific coast, just as it did every year at this time. But nothing in the current climatic conditions or atmospheric configuration could have predicted what he was so anxiously trying to prove on the weather chart spread out over his work bench. He had drawn in purple pencil over the regions involved all the isotherms and isobars he was so familiar with since his days at the Norhausen Geographical Institute on a grant from General José Santos Zelaya's government to study meteorology. It was there he had acquired his knowledge of hurricanes and squalls in the tropics, learned to plot the course of storms and polar winds, and to measure taigas and tundras, all of which experience he distilled in his daily half-page bulletins.

His professor at Norhausen had been none other than Marcus Bjerkner, who had presented him with a signed copy of his *Analysis of Air Masses,* which must also be somewhere in the Observatory, though he had no particular need of it at this moment. No, it was Brückner's book he was looking for, chiefly out of a sense of scientific scrupulousness, because his calculations were perfectly clear, the arrows copied out precisely on his map of Nicaragua. This was a curiosity printed in Belgium at the time of Justino Rufino Barrios' military campaigns in which the Ptolomeic system had been used to trace all the hydrographic details, with all the rivers being charted according to astronomic projections. Though he knew he could always rely on Kaeppen's classification to double-check his results, the margin of possible error would be much greater than if he could find the Beaufort scale.

It was past midnight by now, and he could hear the winds sweeping across the bare cornfield. He could pick each of them out, like someone who can identify each bird by its song in the dark before dawn; to him, they were tame objects which he could not only trap, decipher, and keep track of, thanks to the weather-vane on the Observatory roof, but could also measure the modulation of in his wind-pressure tubes. He was still making a determined search for the book, but now he had set himself the deadline of two in the morning, after which he would reconcile himself to using Kaeppen.

For the first time in many years he turned out all the drawers of his desk, on which stood an anemometer he had brought back from Norhausen that he'd never been able to use because a part was missing. He had written to ask for a spare, but this must have been lost in the vagaries of the war that broke out around that date, and led not merely to the closure of the Institute but also to his finding himself blacklisted and having all his belongings confiscated. It took until 1922 for him to recover his rights and to be appointed the official meteorologist. The Ministry of Education sent abroad for all the instruments needed to set up the Observatory, including a Barren rain-gauge and the biggest hygrometer in Central America; but this the Minister had installed in his own living room, in the belief that it would play music.

From that day to this, the Observatory had been housed in the same pavilion in the middle of a cornfield on the eastern outskirts of the capital. From the outside the wrought-iron spikes of its balcony and the bronzed dome made it look like a refreshments kiosk, while inside it was just like a telegraph office with its signal tappers and belinographs, especially with him standing there in shirt-sleeves with elastic arm-bands, a green eyeshade, and his shirt done up at the neck with a bone collar-stud. At some point, a gravel landing strip for Panaire airplanes had been laid out alongside the building.

At about two the next morning the telephone rang in the guardroom of the presidential palace. A guard cranked the handset to reply.

"This is the meteorological office," said the voice on the line. "Put me through to the President."

"Crazy idiot," the guard muttered. "Can't you find a better time to call?"

"It's very urgent," he insisted.

"Do you realize the trouble you can cause for yourself by disturbing the government?" the soldier warned him, gesturing to an orderly to come over.

"I don't want it said afterwards that I didn't phone him first." The idea of a plot suddenly flitted through the guard's mind. He turned pale. He stammered an excuse and, putting his hand over the mouthpiece, whispered to the orderly to go and fetch the corporal.

"Hold on, don't hang up."

"I'm not going anywhere," came the calm reply.

The corporal was roused from the guard-post. He was convinced right from the start it was something serious.

"Give me your address," he said, "we'll send someone to question you. And whatever you do, stay put."

"But it's the President I want to talk to," the old man insisted impatiently. So then the matter was passed on to the duty officer, and from him to the chief adjutant.

"Look here, whoever you are, there's no question of waking *el hombre* at this time of night; if you have something to say, tell me. I'm his right-hand man."

"The President," he gasped out, "get me the President or I won't be held responsible."

With his chiefs-of-staff, his aides, and his bodyguards clustered around him in the bedroom with its Moorish windows shrouded in muslin curtains, its mirrored wardrobes and tiled floor, the President sleepily stretched out a hand to take the receiver. His tunic was draped over the back of a cane chair next to the bed, and his three-cornered hat and military gaiters lay on the seat.

"Hello, who is that speaking?"

"Is that you, Mr. President, sir?

"Hello?" he repeated, coughing and spluttering into the linen handkerchief held out to him.

"Mr. President, sir, I'm so pleased that you are the first to hear the news."

"Aha," was the only reply, as the President raised his eyebrows at everyone round him.

"Are you still there?"

"Yes, yes: what's all this about?"

"It's going to snow in Nicaragua."

"What?"

"Right now—in December. A cold front with snow is heading for Nicaragua."

The President flung the telephone to the floor and furiously pulled shut the curtains around the four-poster. Then, as though in a Chinese shadow play, he shouted to his guards from behind the lace: "Bring him in."

The bedroom chandeliers snapped out. As he scurried past the print of David's *The Coronation of Napoleon* in the corridor, the adjutant caught the words: "...on bread and water."

He had completed the calculations soon after two, but it

had been closer to four o'clock by the time he got through to the President. At first when he had been cut off he thought it must be a fault on the line, and rang back to the operator. By now day was dawning in Managua: newspaper boys were shouting to sell *La Estrella de Nicaragua*; beggars were already busy sifting through the garbage for food down by the lakeshore; butchers' shops were opening their shutters, and horse-drawn carriages were drawing up in front of the railway station. A delicate smell of bread filled the air, and section after section of the street lighting clicked off. Daylight was pushing its way into the greasy stalls of the Eastside market, into brothels and gambling dens. It touched Dambach hill, the houses in the block halfway up near the tree, and the carts filling the square; reached the Candelaria neighborhood, with marimba music on the Voz de la Victoría, the telephone wires outside the dollar exchange thronged with swallows, and the deserted Hotel Lupone—all the while he stood there clutching the typed pink form to read to the President. "...Northwesterly winds averaging 0.12 on the Kaeppen scale will combine with the effects of the winter solstice in the region of the equator to produce a fall of snow due to the rapid cooling of the lower levels of the atmosphere and an increase in the diameter of the ice crystals in the upper cirrus clouds. Despite being approximately 30° from the equator, parts of Nicaragua will receive considerable amounts of snow around Christmas. More precise details will become available as the winds from the polar regions draw closer...." The whole report took up two typed pages.

It was after a cable arrived from Washington that the

Director of the Meteorological Observatory was taken from his cell in the Fifth Police Station and brought before the President. It contained a report from the US weather ship *Emile* in the Atlantic, according to which on the previous day, December 14th, they had calculated that freezing winds from the Arctic would reach the Pacific coastline of Central America in the days around Christmas. After further consultations between the ship and the weather research bureau in Norfolk, Virginia, the precise co-ordinates had been worked out and disclosed to UPI, which put out the first news report from New York on the morning of December 15th.

"Sit down, won't you?"

The bone collar-stud had come off; he looked dishevelled and unshaven. He was also apparently barefoot.

"What's this you were saying about snow...?"

"It is going to snow in Nicaragua," he said, quietly but firmly.

"Yes, yes, we know that—read this."

"That's precisely what I worked out," he replied after glancing through the report, "except that they did their calculations by extrapolation."

"Right. And how did you do yours?"

The old man delved into the back pocket of his white trousers and pulled out the folded pink sheets.

"It's all here," he said, handing his forecast to the President, who was ensconced behind a desk huge as a catafalque, with lion's paws for feet and the arms of the republic embossed on its side. The aide intercepted the papers and, saluting, passed them on the President.

"Where did you study all this stuff?" he asked, leafing through the report.

"At the Norhausen Institute in Germany."

"When was that?"

"Before the First World War."

"And this is the first time you've managed to discover this snow thing?"

"But this is the first time it has happened, sir."

"Ah, well, yes, I realize that."

The President asked for a light, and was brought a big bronze lighter in the shape of an imperial eagle.

"Look here," he said, raising the golden cigarette holder to his lips. "In my opinion we'd better keep quiet about this. Let them sort the matter out as they think fit; we'll just wait and see."

Every word the President uttered was typed out with two fingers by his private secretary. The President laid the cigarette holder down on an ashtray and folded his hands across his stomach. He was wearing a linen suit and Prussian boots.

"Excuse me, but..." the old man put in.

"As I see it," the President continued, "we pretend we know nothing. You go back to your laboratory and let our friends in the North announce the news of what's going to happen...you follow me?"

"Do you follow him?" the aide echoed, leaning over him. The old man shook his head.

"Look, this is a question of international relations, and they're for me to deal with. So, let's say that officially it was the United States who discovered that it's going to snow: OK?" he said, struggling up out of the heavy red silk-lined chair. "You're free to go." With that, he made for a hidden door, which led out into the gardens. "And I want the day itself declared a national holiday," he called out to his secretary. Then he vanished.

The President made a very moving speech at the traditional switching-on of lights on the huge Christmas tree outside the presidential residence. He wished everyone a white Christmas. Despite a torrid breeze from the lake, the female guests sat on their folding chairs wrapped in woolen shawls or fur coats with matching muffs, while the men perspired in heavy overcoats and scarves. "The day will soon arrive, according to our friends in the North, when snow will fall on us like a blessing from the heavens. Then there will truly be no reason left for us to envy the advanced nations of the old world and of North America." The special American envoy smiled, the President pulled the lever, and the tree was bathed in light.

"I told them not to bother with any artificial frost," the First Lady explained to her husband as they sped away in a cloud of dust on their sleigh. "We'll soon be getting the real thing anyway."

Over the next few days, workmen outdid themselves in efforts to build chimneys on all the smart homes. Panaire planes flew in birch-tree logs from New Hampshire, California apples, frozen turkeys from Miami, and winter clothes, skis, and electric blankets for the stores, which hurriedly installed heating. Carols in English blared from the loudspeaker vans, and everybody scurried along the streets in garish sweaters and hats, peering up at the sky. They had all read in the newspapers that the first sign of snow would be when the white clouds merged into a heavy solid overcast sky like that before a rainstorm.

"Good morning, Señora Vizquez," they would say.

"Oh, Señora Rodriguez, isn't it a beautiful day?"

"You'll soon see how cold it gets."

"Goodness," they laughed excitedly, hurrying into the shops just to try out their heating.

And yet, as the day drew nearer (the weather ships had confirmed it as December 24th), the heat became increasingly unbearable. The atmosphere was stifling; children suffocated in sweaters; all over Managua people sat out on the sidewalks in their rocking chairs, waiting for some sign from the dazzling heat of the sky that beat so intensely down on the road surfaces that it made them drowsy. Deprived of snow, the city lay like a skeleton, decked out in fancy lanterns, with Christmas lights on every street and wreaths on the front doors of houses whose chimneys sent smoke drifting up into the haze, while the bells on the imported sleighs jingled as they turned the corners.

Back in the Observatory, the old man had abandoned his scientific instruments and spent his days sitting on the steps in the glorious sunshine reading back issues of the *International Weather Observer* for the second half of 1929. Occasionally, he would smile absent-mindedly out at the cornfield, as flocks of swallows circled the Observatory roof and settled on the weathervane.

On Christmas Eve, the President, his ministers, the chiefs-of-staff, the diplomatic corps, and the other official guests all took their seats in the grandstand for the start of the spectacle. By decree, as soon as the first flakes of snow began to fall, all the church bells were to be rung, fire sirens and car horns to be sounded. Even the ice cream men were to ring the bells on their carts. The President had prepared a special speech. He sat in the front row, sweltering beneath an immense mink coat (a gift from the Canadian Embassy), a plaid rug across his knees and an astrakhan hat on his head. By six in the evening, though, the heat showed no sign of abating, and several of the ambassadors had drifted away. Strings of yellow lights had come on in the streets, and the music and fireworks from neighborhood processions could be heard from all sides— people were celebrating Christmas as they always had.

"What time was this thing supposed to happen?" the President wanted to know.

"Between three and five p.m., according to the latest report from New York."

"What news since then?"

"We cabled Norfolk, but there was no reply. The operator said they were already closed because it's Christmas Eve."

"Is there nothing we can do?"

"I'm afraid not, sir."

"Somebody's going to pay for this," the President muttered. Then he barked out to his aide: "Get that old fool here again."

By the time the meteorologist appeared, only the members of his cabinet were still alongside the President. The stand in the main square opposite parliament looked as forlorn and deserted as those erected for an early morning parade, which by nightfall no longer arouse any interest even among the street sweepers.

"So you claimed it was going to snow?"

"It *is* snowing," the old man smiled back at him.

"Do you realize I can have you thrown back in jail? I'll charge you with conspiracy to mock the supreme power of the state. That's what I'll charge you with, you'll see."

"My forecast was correct. You never allowed me to show you my final calculations. It is snowing in Nicaragua, but not here."

"Sit down," came the order. "What exactly do you mean?"

"They miscalculated the directional flow of the cold fronts and their area of divergence."

"Speak in plain language, can't you?" the President said, slapping the old man's knee. He had removed his fur coat, and was cooling himself with a palm fan.

"The best thing for you to do is go back to your palace. It will never snow here in Managua—not today or any other day. I calculate it must be snowing at this precise moment over on the Atlantic coast, somewhere in the north."

People were starting to arrive at the Cathedral for midnight Mass.

"You're under arrest anyway. Don't worry, it's only a precaution. We'll see what's happened by tomorrow morning."

The presidential sleigh returned empty to the stables through the back streets of the capital. The President and his wife were driven home in a limousine. They did not even risk travelling in the ceremonial carriage for fear it would be mistaken for the sleigh, since both of them were horse-drawn and had the national flag draped over the driver's seat.

"I was rounding up cattle near the River Mayales," José Lopez, a 45-year-old peasant, told UPI, "when I saw a kind of rain of cotton balls falling from the sky. The cattle stampeded with the cold, and soon the whole plain was covered in a white blanket.''

According to reports reaching the capital from local telegraph offices, the snow affected the mountainous, high-rainfall areas of Nicaragua across a region comprising the Atlantic coast jungles, the broad rivers flowing into the Caribbean, the towns and villages situated to the east of Lake Nicaragua, and the central ranges stretching north from Isabelia. During last night and this morning the temperature in Juigalpa fell to five degrees below zero. Continuous sleet was falling on La Concordia, San Pedro de Lóvago and Santo Tomás; in Acoyapa and Comalapa temperatures ranged between minus five and minus fifteen degrees. The north, including Palacaguina and Yalí, was suffering Arctic conditions, and Mount Chipote had a thick covering of snow. The temperature fell to minus 12 in the Terrabona region, and to minus 15 in Curinguás, where many animals died of hunger and the cold. It was still snowing in Amerrizque and Prinzapolca, and the River Escondido had frozen over, blocking river traffic. The villages of Telpaneca, San Juan del Norte, Wiwilí and Malacatoya were all cut off by snowdrifts.

In Yeluca, Oculí, and La Libertad, the inhabitants stared out of their houses in silent wonder at the falling snow; many of them went to church to pray. "It's like being in the movies," one of the villagers said, laughing.

Several persons were reported to have died from the extreme cold, and the supreme government set up an emergency relief committee.

River birds wheeled with pitiful cries over the frozen mirror of the Siquia. Nicaragua is white.

1968

To Jackie with All Our Heart

The news that Jacqueline Kennedy was to visit Nicaragua caused a great commotion in our smartest circles. What passes for high society felt both immensely flattered and at the same time confused, left in the dark as to the whens, wheres, and hows, that is, when Jacqueline (Jackie, to us) would be setting foot on our soil, where she would be accommodated, how her reception was to be organized. Our welcome would have to be worthy of her, not merely because of her public stature—someone who had been the wife of an historic president, slain by an assassin's bullets; a former first lady of the most powerful nation on earth, who had turned her stay in the White House into a real-life fairy tale; married now to a boundlessly wealthy magnate—but also because of her own personal warmth and charm, her qualities as a woman who has borne suffering with great dignity. No one must be allowed to accuse us of failing to show her the most exquisite hospitality.

So it came about that we members of the Virginia Country Club, an exclusive society founded by North American and Nicaraguan shareholders (its first president, back in the year 1923, being Colonel Glenn J. Andrews, a true-blue Virginian who married Amadita Balcáceres del

Castillo, from one of Granada's most renowned families, the Colonel then staying on in Nicaragua despite repeated requests for him to return to Washington following his outstanding military career in the fight against the Sandinista hordes in the Segovia Mountains, he stayed on, as I said, selecting his friends with unerring taste and devoting his time to growing tobacco, in accordance with the family tradition back in Oakdale, Virginia, and the year in which he was married he called together a group of his closest friends and challenged them: Say, there's no country club here, or am I wrong? When they all shook ther heads, he went on: Let's get to work then; and so the name of Colonel Andrews, founder-president of the Virginia Country Club, became immortal—you can see it on the plaque over the entrance to the stables, the first building given over exclusively to equitation, something we Nicaraguans were all but ignorant of until then) resolved that it should be us who took on the responsibility for organizing Jackie's official welcome, bestowing honors on her, arranging receptions, and so on. In my capacity as secretary to the board of the Virginia Country Club (a position to which I have repeatedly been re-elected since 1953), I called an emergency meeting. It was held in my residence, there being no time to transfer to the Club, which is about eight miles outside Managua by the time one gets a glimpse of the golf fairways from the highway (their grass so well-tended you would think you were in another country). When we were all assembled, it was like having a bucket of cold water poured over us to learn from our past president (who is always invited to board meetings, since we feel we can benefit from his experience) that perhaps our laudable efforts were destined to fail (our past president always expresses himself in such a distinguished way; he is a renowned jurist, a lawyer acting on behalf of many of the companies that have invested in our nation: the Light Mine State Co., the Atlantic Pine Co., the Gold and Silver Mine Co.—as his colleagues say, he always gives the impression he is delivering a speech, whereas I am quite the opposite, I am an electro-dynamics engineer, having graduated from Georgetown University in 1950) and that we would be unable to bring our idea to fruition, since other social and recreational organizations had stolen a march on us, had contacted the US Embassy, cabled Jackie's penthouse on Fifth Avenue and the island of Skorpio in Greece, and were now simply awaiting her acceptance. The past president, with his characteristic aplomb, then revealed that it was the Lions Club and the Rotary Club who had beaten us to it, and had the situation under control (as General Abraham Cornejo, a member of the President's household staff and Club treasurer put it) news which, when we thought about it, left us very disappointed, not just because it robbed us of an honor we felt to be ours by right, but also because these so-called service organizations are not really exclusive (being in fact lax as to who they will accept as members), whilst I, as Club secretary of so many years' standing, took it as a personal affront, and vowed: that's not the end of the matter. I calmed down the other members of the board, who were clearly upset and had begun to discuss the matter heatedly. When they had sat down again, I motioned to them to wait while I went into the study to telephone Ralph on his private number (I am one of the few in our country to know it). Thankfully he was at home, in his cottage close to the Virginia, so convenient when of an afternoon I pass by on my way to the

Club, I often drop in for one of the delicious cocktails that Annie his charming wife mixes; and Ralph as friendly as ever asked: what's up, *que es la cosa* (he speaks Spanish with all our Nicaraguan turns of phrase, to hear him nobody could tell whether he was Nicarguan or American, it's only his complexion, his blue eyes and blond hair that give the game away that he is a *gringo,* as he jokingly describes himself); in his usual obliging way he insisted on talking to me in Spanish, though I feel quite at home in English, thanks to my education, my professional contacts, and because it is one of the two official languages used in the Virginia (the second being Spanish).

I told him about Jackie's visit, which he already knew of anyway; of course, he confided, Annie and Jackie used to be dear friends, classmates at Trinity College, Massachusetts, and though they haven't seen each other for some time, they still have a high regard for each other. Do you know how we came to miss out on John's inauguration in January 1961? It was all due to a slip-up by the protocol services; they lost our address and sent the invitation to another Mr and Mrs Ralph Fridemann who didn't even live in Baltimore, Maryland, on the threshold of the diplomatic world, as we did: yet they were the lucky recipients, and they it was who took the places meant for us—reserved by Jackie herself. What a crying shame, I replied. I know for a fact it's true, Ralph is on intimate terms with presidents and their families—I've seen a portrait signed by Lyndon B. Johnson, no less, on the mantelpiece in Ralph's living room (at the official request of the US Embassy, the owner of the house had a fireplace installed for Ralph, with plastic wooden logs and concealed red lights, which give the impression that the fire is burning all the time); a large framed photograph showing Mr Johnson, his right hand resting on the back of a chair, the other at his waist, and that stern, intelligent, resolute look of his so typical of the man who ruled the destiny of the Free World, and on it a handwritten dedication: "To Mr Ralph Fridemann and his wife, for their high services on behalf of our nation, truly yours, Lyndon B. Johnson, President of the United States of America". Every time I get up and go over to the fireplace, cocktail in hand, to admire the portrait, Ralph smiles at me: "Don't worry, *mano* (he's also served in Mexico), it's authentic, believe me". I nod and think: the day Ralph and his wife come home for dinner, I'll make a point of showing them the diploma and the colored photo of himself which His Holiness Pope Pius XII gave my mother to commemorate her pilgrimage to Rome, at a private audience in the Sistine Chapel, so they can see what the Pontiff wrote in his own hand, in Gothic script and in Spanish (popes can speak at least fourteen languages), a sort of open letter in which he blesses all my family even in the hour of their death—the only reason he did not sign it personally being that he had a bad bout of arthritis at the time, so he asked Cardinal Camarlengo to do it on his behalf.

Yes, I know all about the visit, Ralph told me, not only from the coded messages arriving at the Embassy, but also because Jackie wrote Annie an affectionate little note, but he had heard nothing about any other clubs getting in first, and didn't believe it: anyway, I was not to worry, he would fix it so that all the celebrations would be taken care of by the Virginia Country Club (which after all was founded to provide a permanent link between our two fraternal nations, I quickly reminded him). Yes, he replied, there's no problem, don't worry about it, *che* (Ralph has also been based in Argentina), so I returned to the living room: it's all settled, I told them. What do you mean, asked Freddy? he's the most senior member of the board, and always the least trusting (I suppose he's rather jealous of my success, since all the weight of the Club falls on my shoulders—our social events, garden parties, golf tournaments, and so on) everything's settled, I repeated, I've got it all sewn up (General Cornejo beamed at me, delighted I was speaking his kind of language). Jackie will come straight from the airport to a special reception at our Club; that same evening, there is to be a gala banquet exclusively for our members and their families; the following lunch time, a picnic will be held in the Club grounds, and that afternoon a high-fashion tea with our members' wives and daughters: there won't be any time left for so much as a meow from any other club. Everyone burst out laughing at this ironic dig at the Lions, and they started to slap my back, hug me, and sweep me off my feet in their enthusiasm: I could scarcely breathe, and so many glasses fell to the floor that Maria Eugenia peeped over the upstairs bannister to find out what was going on. She disappeared again with a contented smile as soon as she heard the reason: she knows how to share my triumphs. In the middle of this hubbub, our past president suddenly enquired: "Who did you talk to then?" All the others fell silent, interrupted their congratulations, then pressed me anxiously: "Yes, who did you talk to?"

"To the Ambassador," I reassured them, "To the Ambassador of the United States." Well then, everything is sure to be all right, they shouted and laughed, even more delightedly, and the bravos and backslapping started up again. Sometimes a white lie is justified, because even though the truth is that Ralph is not the Ambassador, but holds an important administrative position—Chief Clerk, as he writes on the order forms he sends out to companies for the purchase of all the Embassy needs in the way of candles, paper clips, stationery, pencils, and so on, nonetheless it is also true that he is worthy of representing his great nation. The thing was to create an impression with my words, and they did have the desired effect: as the others were leaving and starting up their cars I could hear them singing my praises, chuckling as they congratulated themselves on having me on the board. And it was a contrite past president who took me aside as he was going and said: "Forgive me, old boy, it appears I was misinformed." I made light of the whole thing and replied with a laugh: "Think nothing of it, Dan; to err is human—you had the good of the Club at heart." (And I've no wish to boast, but I'm one of the few in this country on first-name terms with him.)

As promised, Ralph set to work on our behalf, but since his efforts were shrouded in secrecy, it was some weeks before I found out what direction they were taking. According to him, we should make no attempt to get in touch with Jackie ourselves, in order not to jeopardize his efforts. We did learn some details about her visit, though, and they took us by surprise: she would be arriving by sea on board her private yacht for a stopover during a world tour, but it had not yet been finally decided which port she would land at in Nicaragua. This made it necessary to call another board meeting, and to get on the telephone again to Ralph. He told me we had no need to worry, our plans wouldn't be affected in the slightest: Jackie could be whisked by

helicopter from her yacht to our golf course—but I didn't
think this was a very good idea, and between my call to
Ralph and the meeting I hit upon another solution, which
everyone agreed was marvellous as soon as I put it to them
(even I was surprised at how the idea had flashed into my
mind). Why not purchase a yacht of our own, sail out in
it to meet Jackie, draw alongside, and have her transfer
from one ship to the other whenever there was a cocktail
party, reception or tea in her honor? That way there
wouldn't be any risk of anyone else intercepting her after
she had landed. They clapped so hard I had to break off—
then, I went on, once we spy her yacht, we can perform
a sort of mock boarding, firing broadsides of bunches of
our native flowers, then calling on her by loudhailer to
surrender. What better than to spare her the noise and
bustle of the city with its dirt and heat, and the common
people who would be sure to mob her, and all the school-
children who would pester her for her autograph? If we
followed my plan, she could be sure of the warmest
welcome, would meet only persons of her own social
standing—and yet everything would be taking place within
Nicaragua, since both ships would be anchored in our
territorial waters, with ours flying the national flag from
its topmast, fluttering in the breeze. These last words caused
a sensation; the others could scarcely contain their joy, and
our wives, who had been chatting in the other room, came
in to share our excitement.

There wasn't the slightest doubt, they whispered, as
to who was going to be the president of the Virginia
Country Club, and for many, many years.

I mustn't forget to mention that one of our biggest
problems was not being sure which port had been chosen

for Jackie's arrival since if we had known, our plan to intercept her yacht on the high seas would have been far more straightforward. According to Ralph, we couldn't know—not only was such information classified, but if by chance the name of the port were leaked, this would be deliberately false, and at the last minute the ship would head elsewhere. Therefore, in my capacity as the person delegated to supervise everything on the board's behalf, I decided to press on as before; I planned for us to embark as the time of Jackie's arrival drew near (this much Ralph promised he would secretly inform me of); we would travel up the coast for a few days, and when Jackie's yacht hove into view we would set out full steam ahead to greet her. This plan also had the advantage of offering our Club members and their relatives an unforgettable cruise.

I was about to fall contentedly to sleep one night shortly before leaving for the United States to purchase our boat (which would need to be of considerable size, seeing there were 450 members, counting residents and associates, plus their families, the crew, service personnel, musicians, etcetera, making a grand total of at least 1500 people to accommodate) when the thought suddenly struck me: which of the oceans will Jackie's yacht be arrving by? I cursed myself—you idiot, you've taken it for granted all along that the yacht will be coming from the Pacific side, but doesn't it make more sense, since it will have started out in the Mediterranean, for it to reach the Atlantic coast, and take us all unawares by putting in at Bluefields? I leapt out of bed, and even though it was three in the morning, I called Ralph to explain my fears to him. Oh, don't worry, he said, we'll know that in plenty of time, so your boat can be waiting in the right spot. Then he hung up, leaving me with the distinct impression that he had answered half-asleep, but when I kept on about it over the following days, he finally relented and revealed (at the risk of being accused of high treason) that her yacht would be reaching Nicaragua via the Pacific, passing through the Panama Canal en route from the US Virgin Islands. I really appreciated him for that. Only a true friend would take that kind of risk, I thought, so off I went to New Orleans with my mind at rest to inspect the boats on offer. None of these was brand-new, but they were in excellent condition, according to the descriptions given us by the naval brokers. When I got there, though, not a single one appealed to me, they were all old and rusty, their plumbing didn't work, the cabins smelled musty, their dance floors had caved in, their swimming pools were a disgrace. I can say with pride that none of them was worth the price we were willing to pay.

I was on the point of flying back to Nicaragua, disheartened at not having found any suitable vessel, to raise with the other board members a proposal I had received from Japan, when an agent telephoned me from San Francisco, California, offering for sale no less a ship than the *Queen Elizabeth!* Perfectly preserved, almost as immaculate as on the day of her launch, she was now anchored in the bay there, where they planned to convert her into a luxury hotel. Immensely excited at the prospect, I agreed to go and have a look. I thought to myself, Good God, what a feat it would be to buy a liner like that! The Virginia Country Club buys the *Queen Elizabeth* to welcome Jacqueline Kennedy in!

Once there, everything worked like a charm. I toured the liner (my mother had sailed on her for her trip to Rome) and was entranced. What a stupendous jewel, what indescribable splendor, a veritable floating palace, a city sailing the seas (phrases which, I have to confess, I read in the publicity brochures I was given by the salesman); how magical it was to gaze on her twelve decks, literally dozens of shops, ten theatres, ten cinemas, fourteen ballrooms, ice skating and water skiing rinks, her fifteen swimming pools, eight tennis and four squash courts, ten croquet greens, her three thousand luxury state rooms, five chapels each catering for a different religion, bars on all sides, gaming rooms, solariums, casinos: in short, all that one could possibly wish for. The asking price was by no means excessive, considering what such a colossus would mean to us, so I at once got in touch with my colleagues back in Nicaragua and, after three weeks' messages, talks and bargaining, the money had been raised, and our country's most respected banks, solidest finance houses, most distinguished industrial and agricultural concerns (all of them headed by Club members) had agreed to act as guarantors. Last but not least, in a gesture that really touched me, all the Club's share capital as well as its premises, grounds, playing courts and installations, were mortgaged to cover the purchase. This left the Virginia committed to the hilt, but the deal was signed in the captain's suite on board the ship itself, on what was for me an historic evening. I must stress that all our members fully realized from the outset what this step meant: glory, the definitive consecration of our beloved Club. We were paying a small price indeed for what was the outstanding social event of the year, of the whole century, not just in Central America and the Caribbean but in all Latin America. We would make news in the United States itself, where our names would be etched in gilt for ever more in the annals of the jet-set; *Time* magazine would have to mention us in its celebrated "People" section, and perhaps, when my time was up, my own name would appear among its "Milestones".

Naturally, I made the return journey to Nicaragua on board the *Queen Elizabeth*, crewed by a full complement and with her former captain at the helm—the same man who only a short while before had told me with tears in his eyes that he thought he would be steering his ship to her grave.

Never before had a liner of such size and splendor docked at a Nicaraguan port, and so our arrival turned into a national holiday, with thousands of people thronging the port of Corinto to give me one of the most memorable days of my life. I was the sole passenger, the one who had thought up this fabulous scheme, the man who had fulfilled our members' wildest ambitions. Nobody now would dare suggest that Nicaragua was not going to receive Jacqueline Kennedy in a manner befitting her; there was the *Queen Elizabeth*!

According to Ralph, there was little more than two months left before she arrived, so there was no time to waste: the personal fortunes of our richest members went towards refitting the ship for the occasion. Furniture, drapery, lighting, cutlery, dinner services, clocks, mirrors, carpeting were all freighted in by plane. Hundreds of foreign experts built new sports courts, refurbished the swimming pools, inspected the plumbing and wiring, the background music, the refrigerators and the kitchens, while the liner was stocked with copious supplies of drink, meat, game, shellfish, vegetables, fruit, cereals, preserves. It may be worth remarking that all this came from the United States—as did the waiters (specialists in sea cruises), the musicians, the chefs, florists, hairdressers, and masseurs. Our only worry was that, alongside our *Queen Elizabeth,* Jackie's yacht might look very tiny, but in all truth we didn't think this would upset her.

For the next few weeks I became (it would be false modesty to deny it) one of the most important people in the country. The President of the Republic invited me to all his receptions, and regaled me with private dinners, merely in order to suggest to me the name of some minister or official he thought should be invited. As there was plenty of room to spare on the *Queen Elizabeth* even after our members and their families had been taken care of, we were offering cabins for the cruise, with the right of entry to all the festivities being held in Jackie's honor. We received thousands of requests, all of which we checked carefully, setting up a points system to avoid all argument. A week before the trip we were still sifting through more than three thousand requests, although fewer than fifty berths were still available. Tickets were fetching up to ten thousand dollars on the black market, but the Club would have nothing to do with this speculation, and sold all ours at the publicly announced price. There was such a fierce struggle to secure a place that I remember there were scuffles and fights, insults in the newspapers and even shooting incidents—all of which explains why the President of the Republic was so eager to use his influence on me, (since it was I who in the last resort decided who should get a ticket) and to get me to consider his cronies—particularly those in the armed forces, most of whom we would never allow as members of our Club.

I must say we aroused a tremendous amount of jealousy. We were attacked personally, our homes and cars were stoned, marches and protest meetings were organized against us, and there were strike threats in our factories and businesses—all, in my opinion, out of resentment from those who couldn't get a place on the *Queen Elizabeth*, whether because those behind these repugnant demonstrations had insufficient funds, or because their applications were turned down as unsuitable. We were snubbed, slandered behind our backs; but was it our fault if (as rumor had it) entire families had sold their possessions and taken out crippling loans just so they could join the trip?

At last the great day arrived. At last we embarked. On the quayside to see us off were bands specially hired by the Club, and young girls with baskets of flowers (also paid for by the Club). The national anthems of the United States, Nicaragua, and Greece (which I must admit I didn't know) were played; the flags were hoisted, and we set sail. Ralph and Annie did not come with us. That is something which to this day I cannot fathom: they did not appear at the dockside at the appointed time, even though the previous day I had gone especially to their house to give them the pleasant surprise that they were to accompany us as the Club's guests of honor (Ralph had somehow never got around to becoming a member), and that, since she was such a close friend of Jackie's, we had decided Annie should have the honor of presenting her, on behalf of the Club, with a huge heart of red flowers with the inscription in gold letters:

TO JACKIE, WITH ALL OUR HEART
an honor which, though it really corresponded to the Club president's wife, I had succeeded in arranging for Annie in order to show Ralph how grateful I was for all he had done. Annie got very embarrassed and upset (poor thing,

who wouldn't?); she took Ralph aside and I could hear them whispering. When they came back over to me, they said of course they would love to come, though both of them had turned pale, with emotion I suppose, and perhaps it was because of the shock I gave them that they did not turn up; anyway here we are still at sea, life has become downright boring, day follows day, it seems we've been steaming up and down this coast for months, staring at the smoke from distant volcanoes, or the vegetation, the lights of tiny ports, watching night fall, watching the rain, growing tired of always the same music, the same games; our food is rationed now, our members are gloomy and all their families are completely fed up, but Jackie cannot fail us, so we go on sailing from one sea lane to another searching for a trace of smoke from her ship on the horizon, we're convinced she must come, and every dawn brings us renewed hope that this will be the day for celebration, for resounding trumpets, for the heart of red flowers, because Jackie has to reach the coast of Nicaragua eventually—I can't bear even to think of how dreadful it would be to go back and confront our enemies' smirking faces; whenever I meet the other board members on deck with their woeful expressions I give them a look that says: I for one will never go back.

1971

Saint Nikolaus

for Dorel

The moment Frau Schleting came towards him, arms outstretched, to get him to dance, he knew it was the start of the disaster he had feared all evening but now was powerless to avoid.

If only he could have taken his 100 mark fee and left as soon as he had finished his job, by now he would have been back in the dank loneliness of his room, smoking his last Krone before wrapping himself in the quilt that was falling apart at the seams, to go to sleep with no greater fear than that the dull routine of his days would go on unchanged.

The first complication had been the sheer size of the pile of presents. He had spent close to an hour helping the boy unwrap the parcels, and they had still done fewer than half. The child's fascination had given way to disinterest, and he was dozing in the middle of a profusion of toys, wrapping paper, boxes and ribbons when Herr Schleting carried him off to bed.

But that hadn't really been the cause—he might even so have got his money and left the house, walked down into the U-Bahn at Viktorie-Louise-Platz, and have been in his room before it had begun to snow. Yes, he muttered to himself as he listened to the measured but inexorable tread of footsteps coming up the stairs: it was Frau Schleting who had brought on the disaster.

A hundred marks would ease a lot of his worries, he had said to himself the night before when Petrus, the bar-man in *Los Nopales,* had suggested the kind of job that anyone in his position would have been glad to accept: there were still a few vacancies for Santa Clauses to go and enter-tain rich children in their homes on Christmas Eve. Petrus' girlfriend worked in the Kantstrasse employment agency and could arrange everything.

That morning, when he arrived at the agency, she had whispered a warning that this wasn't really a job for foreigners, still less for people who looked Latin American or Turkish: they always preferred white, ruddy-cheeked men. But since she was on his side, she wouldn't mention that at all to them, and gave him the address and telephone number: Barbarossastrasse 19/II, in Wilmersdorf: Herr and Frau Schleting. Ring beforehand to sort out the details.

By noon, he still didn't have a Santa Claus costume, and realized he was going to have to ask Krista if she'd lend him the 50 marks he needed to hire the suit and put down a deposit. When he went to look for her at her work in the tiny basement stationer's shop of the Europa Center, she had answered in her habitual gruff voice, hoarse from cigarette smoking and thickened still further by her feigned anger, that yes she would lend him the money, but that this was the very last favor she would ever do him.

Fifteen years earlier, when he had arrived in Berlin from Maracaibo to study electrical engineering at the Technical University, thanks to his father's snobbish desire to see his son a graduate engineer from Germany, one of his first misfortunes had been to meet Krista, who then was working as a cashier in the Goethe Institute.

He never mentioned Krista in the long letters he wrote his father attempting to explain his repeated failures as a student, but if he had to put the blame on anyone, it would have been her, not because she really was the culprit, but simply because she had been a part of his life here from the very beginning. And when eventually he gave up attending the university, and with his father's death had begun to scratch a living as a waiter or a stand-in musician in pizzerias and Latino restaurants, Krista was still around, sitting all alone at her table, slowly sipping her beer (even though lately they scarcely exchanged a word) and slowly wasting away in her pursuit of him.

The tiny costume rental shop in Karl Marxstrasse, in Neuköln, had only one Santa Claus outfit left, which didn't fit him. In recent years he had acquired a paunch just like his father's, but the suit was far too tight, even though he imagined Santa Clauses ought to be decidedly rotund, which he certainly wasn't. The red flannel trouser legs left a wide expanse of calf exposed, and worse still, the boots weren't included in the outfit, so he would have to turn up in his worn-out winter shoes.

But finally, hours earlier on this Christmas Eve, he had donned the costume and walked down the stairs of the nondescript, grey building identical to so many others along the Manitusstrasse in the outlying workers' district of Kreuzberg, overrun these days by Turkish immigrants, who crowded the streets gesticulating like characters in silent movies and set up their stalls on the sidewalks or under the bridges.

His footsteps echoed like hammerblows down the endless wooden staircase. As he stepped out into the yard, in whose lofty walls only an occasional lighted window shone, gusts of icy wind stung his face beneath the shiny strands of the false beard. Side by side in the darkness of the yard, the frozen rubbish bins resembled a row of tombstones.

Trying hard to conceal the red suit under his overcoat, he had walked along the Maybach Ufer as stealthily as a burglar, but the cold made his hand shake so much that the tinkling of his bell gave him away in spite of himself to the rare passers-by who scurried along the street and rushed into the dark doorways. He left behind the black waters of the canal with its reflections of the street lamps in the night still free of snow, and made his way down into the Kottbusser Tör U-Bahn.

The station platform was deserted apart from a tiny, smartly-dressed old lady, who at first stared at him in amazement, then smiled pleasantly to show she had understood. He walked past her to the furthest of the brightly lit, empty yellow cars that had just pulled up in front of them with a drawn-out gentle sigh.

The train moved off in the direction of Nollendorf-Platz, where he had to change. As so often before, the giants on the station advertisements flashed in front of him. He knew that, though in the end the passengers were swallowed up by the darkness of the tunnels, *they* remained up there in their multicolored Valhalla, their confident smiles like disdainful sneers, a constant reminder of how insignificant was his passage through the stations on his daily journeys in those same yellow trains, set against their happy, triumphant permanence high on the walls. Once again he was dazzled by the vision of a girl with magnificent hair smoking a cigarette, the same girl who through the days of summer, when a clinging smell of dog shit filled the Berlin air, stared defiantly out at the world as she hung from the rigging of a white yacht. Now, as he slipped into the tunnel, she had on a pair of skis and was looking haughtily out from a perfect, snowy landscape, so bursting with happiness her eyes were gleaming mercilessly: *gut gelaunt geniessen.*

He felt for the packet of Krone inside the Santa Claus jacket that reeked of mothballs. A cough followed in the lonely train car, his chronic racking cough from all those icy winters. He was down to his last three cigarettes. He felt for them simply to reassure himself they still existed, that they hadn't already become part of his past, because until the night before he had been getting a packet of Krone every day in *Los Nopales* out of the money he earned playing the drums for the Caribbean group that appeared there.

Los Nopales was a dive in Carmenstrasse frequented by students. In spite of its name, the only thing Mexican about it was a dusty wide-brimmed sombrero pinned to a Mexican blanket above the bar. The previous evening the police had closed the place down for reasons of hygiene, and Petrus, as he was paying him off, had handed him a final packet of Krone together with a few marks. There's no chance of you lot working as Santa Clauses, Petrus had joked to the Caribbean musicians as they snapped shut their instrument cases in the gloom and made their way out through the kitchen door. The blacks had all shaken their heads, highly amused.

The shops in the Viktorie-Louise-Platz loomed in the darkness, their neon lights extinguished on this silent Christmas Eve. As he crossed the rough cobbles of the square trying to find Barbarossastrasse, he could feel both his big toes poking out of the holes in the thick pair of socks.

A wave of anger swept over him at the scratchy false beard, at his nagging cough, at his absolute certainty that he would never return to Maracaibo. His father's death, which meant an end to the stream of letters that had brought him good humor, enthusiasm, a never-failing check, and an unswerving optimism that one day he would be an engineer despite the passing of the years, also meant that all his connections with his family had ceased, apart from an occasional letter from his two sisters, who were married to genuine engineers. They wrote to him, with a mixture of affection and scorn, as ''the German'', in a distant echo of his father's former cheerfulness.

Then when he had rung the doorbell, he met Herr Schleting, who was impeccably dressed in a black dinner suit, the very image of one of those mature, dignified giants who advertised Jägermeister brandy: *Der Deutsche mit dem freundlichen Akzent.* Over his shoulder he could see, not a wretched evil-smelling hole like his own, with books piled in heaps in the corners, rolls of useless plans, and tourist posters of Venezuela as the only decoration, but instead a supernaturally lit living room, just like those of the billboard giants, a seemingly endless mansion whose spaciousness was extended infinitely by mirrors, white walls, crimson curtains, marble fireplaces, and crystal chandeliers, statuettes, flower vases, standard lamps, a vast expanse of carpet: and all this set out as exquisitely as in the Möbel Grünewald ad: *die altmodische Neumode.*

Cautious and diffident, Herr Schleting had smiled and ushered him in with a curt nod of the head. Precisely as they had agreed over the telephone, the little boy was waiting for him seated on the red velvet armchair next to the massive fireplace that had more the air of an altar. Quiet but expectant, wearing a blue corduroy suit, the child must have been given instructions not to budge from the huge pile of blue, red, and gold boxes, which towered almost as high as the glittering Christmas tree.

Herr Schleting had exclaimed, with festive solemnity: ''Santa Claus! Santa Claus!'' and stepped back so that he could begin; but he stood hesitating on the doorstep in stunned bewilderment, not knowing how to start, confronted by the apparition of the boy on his distant throne in the center of this huge advertising poster.

He couldn't recall how or why he had started to laugh strenuously and fling his arms up and down like the toy Santa Clauses in the stores, as the occasion demanded, with every gesture sneaking a look at Herr Schleting, who still stood, smiling imperturbably, in the open doorway. He swaggered over to the boy, at last remembering to ring his bell, and hearing his own deep-throated false laughter as if the sound took a long while to emerge from his throat, where it was a struggle as to whether his wheezing cough or the guffaws would win out.

It was some time later that Frau Schleting had made her appearance. By then he had already started to help the boy unwrap his presents, throwing in the occasional chortle, when suddenly he heard the strains of *Stille Nacht, Heilige Nacht* blaring out. It was then that he had seen her, dancing alone as if in a dream, waving a bottle of Mumm in one hand, a glass high over her head in the other, as she swayed to the rhythm. She was oblivious to Santa Claus' triumphant arrival and to the ceremony of the presents. Just as in the Mumm advertisements, she was dressed in a long, white lace gown, low-cut at the back, her neck and wrists bedecked with jewels: *Mumm, reicher Genuss entspringt der*

Natur.

Herr Schleting had gone discreetly over to turn the music down, then returned to his vantage point for the opening of the presents, but Frau Schleting insisted on turning it up again, and went on dancing with the bottle in her hand. Finally it was Herr Schleting who gave up and allowed her to continue with her Christmas cheer.

When the boy had become drowsy, Herr Schleting motioned politely for him to stop. He asked him to take a seat for a moment while he put his son to bed. All this time Frau Schleting carried on spinning around the room without paying him the slightest attention. She drank from her glass of Mumm, and by now was clapping to the beat of a Bavarian brass band that had replaced the carol.

On his return, Herr Schleting had asked him somberly if he would care for anything to drink and he, spluttering through the troublesome strands of the false beard, had answered automatically that he'd like a beer, not really sure he wanted a drink at all, but feeling that a beer would be the most modest and respectful thing to ask for in all that glittering luxury.

Herr Schleting pulled the green bottle from his sleeve like a magician and ceremoniously poured the Kronbacher out into a long-stemmed glass, much weightier in his hand than it had appeared. Somewhere beyond the glass where the golden beer shone: *mit Felsquellwasser gebraut,* was a greeny-blue pond sketched hazily behind a bank of reeds that swayed gently in the breeze.

Herr Schleting stood, his arms folded in front of him, looking on with the detached air of a scientist as he waited for him to finish his drink. He was swallowing it down as quickly as he could, convinced that as soon as he stood up

Herr Schleting would whisk a gold-tipped leather wallet from his dinner jacket pocket and hand him a brand-new, crisp, hundred-mark note.

With what in all likelihood were intended as his parting words, Herr Schleting had then asked him—pronouncing each word slowly and distinctly as people do when trying to be polite to foreigners, where exactly he came from. How extraordinary! he had said with a hollow laugh, he hadn't spotted his accent at all on the telephone: as if rather than being a compliment to his German, this made it even more amazing and comical, like the Santa Claus hood jammed on the mop of his already greying Afro hair.

It was at this point that Frau Schleting, who had apparently only just realized he was there, came over. That was the start of the disaster. ''My Spanish Santa Claus! Oh, *que viva España*!'' she shouted gaily. From somewhere high above him—she was an uncommonly tall woman— she offered him her slender, bejewelled hand, gripping him vigorously in the handshake, but then letting herself fall onto the sofa so suddenly that for a moment he was scared she might crash on top of him. She swept back her hair and, nibbling at the rim of her glass, stared at him with passionate eyes.

He had no idea how to respond, beyond folding his white-gloved hands over his stomach that bulged in the tight red jacket, and shooting a worried look in the direction of Herr Schleting. The latter, doubtless out of a sense of pro-priety, preferred to pretend he hadn't seen a thing, the only sign of any impatience on his part being the way he drummed the heel of his patent leather shoe on the thick-piled carpet.

Then, with what was an apparently careless gesture,

Frau Schleting had started to run a fingernail up and down his trouser leg, mirroring the movement with her lips round the rim of the glass. He glanced again at Herr Schleting, who this time pursed his lips and shook his head in annoyance.

He had stood up to say good-bye, get his money and leave, but was forcibly held back. She clawed at his arm and made him sit down again, ensnaring him with burning glances. This time, when he collapsed disheartened onto the sofa, there was no need to look over imploringly at Herr Schleting. He at last had begun to rebuke his wife, in his quiet, steely voice: she was not behaving as she should, it was unworthy of her to give a false impression to foreigners like that—stressing the word *foreigners* to emphasize how unthinkable her conduct was; even though the festivities excused a certain amount of goodwill, he begged her to regain her composure. All this accompanied by a tiny stretched smile, yet another demonstration of his unfailing politeness.

It had started to snow. The snow fell silently past the windows; as always, it filled him with delight and wonder, although this didn't in any way lessen his embarrassment at the mess he was in. He was the only one who noticed the snow. Suddenly, Frau Schleting proposed a toast to Christmas and to Spain. Without waiting for her husband to agree, she filled their glasses, the champagne overflowing onto table and carpet.

Bound by the strictures of his courtesy, Herr Schleting stood up and drank. He too was forced to toast, swallowing the champagne as quickly as he had the beer. This merely meant that she filled his glass again, splashing wine down the front of his costume; and each time he emptied it, anxious to be off, she refilled it, serving herself at the same time.

Herr Schleting, who some time before had placed his own glass well out of reach, now slapped his knees as he made to rise. He wished to thank Mister... who must have other appointments to keep, other homes to visit that night, and so it must be time to say farewell. At this Herr Schleting rose to his feet and with the same elegant, unruffled gesture as he had ushered him in, made to show him the door.

How many glasses of Mumm had Frau Schleting plied him with? He hadn't the faintest idea. He had already tossed aside his red hood, so that now it was his bushy Afro hair that Frau Schleting was ogling, chattering all the time about Spain. He lounged back on the sofa, no longer protesting as she continued to fill his glass, guffawing as he tried to explain that he had nothing to do with Spain, and uninvited holding forth about Venezuela—the plains, *Alma Llanera,* the mountains, the people from his hometown Maracaibo, the forest of oil derricks on the lake, the heat, and how you could fry an egg at noon on the pavement in Maracaibo. He was even telling jokes about dictators and Pérez Jiménez, but these didn't even raise the flicker of a smile on Herr Schleting's face.

It was still snowing outside, but by now he hated the idea of this dirty, freezing snow, the slippery surface of the salted pavements, the stale smell of soot in the U-Bahn entrance at Viktorie-Louise-Platz, the dismal lights in the tunnels and the muffled roar of the trains, hated the thought of the eternal smirking giants in their vigil on the walls this Christmas midnight. "Here's to you," he had called out, drinking now in his best carefree manner, spreadeagled on the sofa. He unbuttoned the Santa Claus jacket to feel for a Krone, and his red and grey checked lumberjack shirt spilled out. He asked Herr Schleting for a light.

Never for a second had Herr Schleting appeared taken aback by his impertinence. He merely straightened his bow tie and paced up and down, his arms still folded across his chest. Frau Schleting was stretched out on the sofa, and lay there toying with her empty glass. She had slipped off her shoes, and was tickling him with her toes. Suddenly though, she stirred, leapt up, and asked him if he knew how to dance *Que Viva España!*

To which he had replied laughing that he knew nothing about *pasodobles,* that was for fairies: no, he would teach her to dance *joropos, cumbias, guarachas, mambos.* She would have none of that though—what she wanted was to dance *Que Viva España!* with her Spanish Santa Claus.

Sometime about then Herr Schleting had slipped into the dining room. From there, as he used his lighter to light the candles, he reminded his wife that their traditional Christmas dinner was waiting on the table. He said this in the same even tone, as though there were only the two of them present and nothing untoward had happened. Her only answer was to repeat that she wanted to dance *Que Viva España!* with her Spanish Santa Claus. She staggered over to a pile of records to look for it. He was snorting with laughter—no, she'd got it all wrong, he wasn't Spanish, where on earth had she got that idea? Herr Schleting, as his wife began to shout *Olé! Olé!* warned in the same soft-spoken cool voice that nobody was going to play *Que Viva España!* nobody was going to dance *Que Viva España!*

Que Viva España! burst from the stereo. It was when she swayed over to him, snapping her fingers to the rhythm like a flamenco dancer, that he had realized the disaster was inevitable.

Inevitable when, in spite of being perfectly aware that Herr Schleting had suddenly disappeared from the dining room, he was fool enough to start dancing with her, and let her pull him close and breathe her yeasty breath into his false beard—*uno, dos, uno, dos, olé*!— while she stroked the back of his neck with a bony, bejewelled hand. Even more inevitable when she tried to pull off his beard to kiss him properly, still beating out the *pasodoble* rhythm and frog-marching him in between the furniture.

All at once the lights went out, and the room was lit solely by the scarlet and emerald decorations of the giant Christmas tree. Not only did Frau Schleting fail to sense the danger, but the darkness seemed to excite her still further. She shouted again at the top of her voice: *Que Viva España*! locking him in her embrace. The explosions drowned her shout, and fragments of the huge gilt-framed mirror shattered onto the side tables and armchairs. Herr Schleting was standing in the midst of a cloud of gunsmoke, calmly cradling a double-barrelled shotgun. He caught a glimpse of his green hunter's cap with its countless badges. Frau Schleting, blissfully unaware of the explosions, went on dancing crazily, all alone. He himself was frantically scrabbling on all fours to find his red hood and the false beard—which Frau Schleting had eventually succeeded in pulling off—because he had to return all the items of the costume. As he crawled over to the door two more loud bangs rang out, followed by another two as he fled headlong down the stairs.

Now, back in the damp loneliness of his room in Manitusstrasse he is sitting on the bed smoking his very last Krone. The red flashes from the patrol cars down in the yard spiral up towards his window, lending the frosty windowpanes an oven-like glow. He can hear the hollow sound of the policemen's footsteps as they climb to arrest him for being a foreigner who has disturbed the peace of a German home. The Santa Claus costume is draped over the same armchair in which he has sat for so many years poring over engineering textbooks without ever understanding a thing. Filled with the bitterness and frustration he'll take back with him to Maracaibo, he knows in an instant that he'll be dubbed, with pitying sarcasm: *the German*. Forever.

Managua, November 1984

The Perfect Game

Usually as he rushed out of the tunnel into the stands his eyes went straight to the bullpen to see if the kid was warming up. Had the manager finally decided to use him as starter? Tonight, though, his bus had broken down on the South Highway and he had arrived so late that the Boer-San Fernando game was already well under way. Back in the urine-smelling tunnel he'd heard the umpire's screech of "Strike!" so now, with dinner pail under one arm and bottle under the other, he hurried out into the dazzling whiteness, which seemed to float down like a milky haze from the depths of the starry sky.

He always tried to get to the stadium before the San Fernando manager had handed his team's line-up to the head umpire, while the pitchers were still warming up in the bullpen. Sometimes his son would be one of them, so he would press up against the wire fence, his fingers gripping the wire, to show him he was there, that he had arrived. The boy was too shy to acknowledge his presence, and invariably kept on practising in that silent, ungainly way of his. But by the beginning of the game he had always been back on the bench: never once since San Fernando had signed him for the big league at the opening of the season had he started as pitcher. Some nights he hadn't even warmed up, and he would shake his head at his father from the shadows of the dugout: no, it wasn't going to be tonight either.

And now, just when he had got there so late, he scanned the green of the floodlit field and spotted him at once on the pitcher's mound. There he was, a thin, slightly hunched figure, following the catcher's signals intently. Before his father could put the dinner pail down to adjust his glasses, he saw him wind up and pitch.

"Strike!" he heard the umpire shout a second time in the sweltering night. He peered down again, shielding his eyes with his hand: it was him, his boy was pitching, they'd put him on to start. He saw him casually field the ball the catcher returned to him, then wipe the sweat from his brow with the glove. He still needs a bit of polish, he's still raw, his father thought proudly.

He picked up the dinner pail and, as if frightened of making any noise, walked carefully, almost on tiptoe, to the limit of the cheap seats behind home plate, as close as he could get to the San Fernando dugout. He had no idea of how the game stood. He was aware only that at last his boy was up there on the mound under the floodlights, while out beyond the scoreboard and the stands stretched the vast black night.

He paused as a harmless infield fly floated up. The shortstop took a few steps back, and spread his arms wide to show it was his catch. He caught it safely, threw the ball back to the mound, then the whole team trotted off to the dugout. End of inning. His boy strolled off, staring at his feet.

The stadium was almost empty. There was no applause or shouting, the atmosphere was more like a practice match when a few curious onlookers drift into the stadium and huddle together in tiny groups, as if to keep warm.

Still standing, he looked over at the scoreboard above the brightly colored billboards, high in the stadium beyond the direct light of the floodlights and already half in shadow. The scoreboard itself was like a housefront with windows. The men who hung the figures in the two windows that showed the score for each inning were silhouetted against it. One of these shadows was busy closing the window for the bottom of the fourth inning with a nought.

	1	2	3	4	5	6	7	8	9		H	E
SAN FERNANDO	0	0	0	0							0	0
BOER	0	0	0	0								

Boer hadn't managed to hit against his boy, and his team had made no errors, so he was pitching a perfect game. A perfect game—as he cleaned his glasses, breathing on them then wiping them on his shirt, with the bottle still tucked under one arm and the dinner pail on the floor beside him.

He walked up a few steps to be with the nearest group of spectators. He sat next to a fat man with a blotchy white face who sold lottery tickets. He was surrounded by a halo of peanut shells. He split the shells with his teeth, spat them out, then chewed on the nuts. The father carefully set the dinner pail and the bottle down. He had brought the dinner his wife always prepared for the boy to eat after the game. The bottle was full of milky coffee.

"No runs at all?" he looked back awkwardly to ask the others, to make sure the scoreboard was correct. A stiff neck he'd had for years made it hard for him to turn his head. The fat man looked at him with the easy familiarity of baseball fans. Everybody in the stands knows one another, even if they've never met before.

"Runs?" he exclaimed, as though taken aback by a blasphemy, but still chewing steadily. "They haven't even got to first base with that skinny kid pitching for San Fernando."

"He's only a boy," a woman in the row behind said, pursing her lips in pity as if he really were still a small child. She had gold teeth and wore pebble glasses. Between her feet was a large handbag, at which she kept glancing down anxiously.

Another of the spectators sitting higher up chuckled a toothless grin, "Where the hell did they dig up such a beanpole?" The father struggled to turn his head properly so he could see who was insulting his boy. He fiddled with his glasses to get a clearer view of him and to glare his reproach. One of the sidepieces of his glasses was missing, so he had them tied around one ear with a shoelace.

"He's my son," he announced to the whole group, staring at them defiantly despite the crick in his neck. The gap-toothed heckler still had a sarcastic smile on his face, but didn't say a word. Still spitting out shells, the fat man patted his leg. No runs, no hits, no errors? His son was out there, pitching for the first time, and he had a clean sheet. He felt at home in the stands.

And now he heard on the rumbling loudspeakers that it was his boy who was going out to open the inning for San Fernando. He didn't last long. One of the assistants threw a jacket around his shoulders to keep his arm warm.

"He's no great shakes as a batter," his father explained, to no one in particular.

"There's no such thing as a pitcher who can bat," the woman answered. It was strange to see her without her husband, alone in this group of men. She ought to be at home in bed at that time of night, he thought; but she knows a thing or two about the game. His own wife had never wanted to go with him to the stadium at night. She prepared the boy's food, then sat in the room that served as shoe repair shop, kitchen and dining room, glued to the radio, though she couldn't really follow the action.

The San Fernando team was taking to the field again after getting nothing from their half-inning. His boy was strolling back to the mound. Bottom of the fifth inning.

"Let's see how he does," the fat man grunted affectionately. "I've been a Boer fan all my life, but I take my hat off to a good pitcher." With that, he swept off his yellow cap with its Allis-Chalmer badge in salute.

Boer's fourth batter was the first at the plate. He was a Yankee import, and was chewing gum or tobacco. To judge by the bulging cheek and the way he spat constantly, it must have been tobacco. All his boy needed were three pitches. Three marvellous strikes— the last of them a curve that broke beautifully over the outer edge of the plate. The Yank never even touched it. He looked stunned.

"He didn't see them," the woman laughed. "That kid's growing up fast."

Then there was an easy grounder to the shortstop. The last batter popped out to the third baseman. All three were out in no time.

"Will you look at that," gap-tooth shouted. "That beanpole's no pushover." Too bad there were so few people to hear him. The stands all around them were empty, and he could see only a few cigarette butts glowing down in the reserved seats section under the lights from the radio commentators' boxes. This time he didn't even bother to turn around to the smart-ass. Fifteen outs in a row. Would his wife be beside the radio back home? She must have understood some of it, if only the name of her boy.

The San Fernando team was batting again. The top of the sixth inning. One of them got to first with quick bunt, then the catcher, number five in their line-up, hit a double, and the man on first made a desperate run of the bases and just scraped home. That was all: the top of the sixth was over—with one run on the scoreboard.

"Well," the fat Boer supporter said sadly, "now your boy is one up."

That was the first time he'd called him "your boy". And there he was, strolling out, hunched and frail, back to the mound, his features lengthened under the shadow of his cap. Just a kid, as the woman had said.

"He'll be eighteen in June," he confided to his neighbor, but the fat man was suddenly on his feet cheering, because the ball was flying off the bat out to center-field. His own heart leapt as he saw the ball soaring into the outfield, but over by the billboards, where the lettering glistened as though it had just rained, the centerfielder was running back to make the catch. He collided noisily with the fence, but held the ball. Disappointed, the fat man sat down again. "Good hit," was all he said.

Next there was a grounder behind third base. The third baseman scooped it up behind the bag and threw it as hard as he could. Out at first.

"The team's doing all it can for your boy," the woman said.

"Whose side are you on now, Doña Teresa?" the fat

man asked, annoyed.

"I never take sides. I only come to bet, but today there's nothing going," she replied, unruffled. Her bag was full of money to bet on anything: ball or strike, base hit or error, run or not. And the fat man came to sell his lottery tickets in those little packets.

The third man hit a chopper right in front of the plate. The catcher grabbed it and threw to first. The batter didn't even bother to run. This incensed the fat man.

"What are they paying that chicken for?...Up yours!" he bawled through cupped hands.

Someone strolled down from the deserted stands, a small blue plastic transistor pressed to his ear. The fat man called to him by name, "What does Sucre make of this?"

"He says there's the chance of a perfect game," the man replied, imitating the voice of the famous commentator, Sucre Frech.

"Is that what he says?" the father gasped, his voice thick with emotion. He fiddled with the loop of the shoelace behind his ear, as though that would help him hear better.

"Turn your radio up," the fat man demanded. The other put it down on the ground and turned it louder. The fat man lifted his hand in an automatic gesture of throwing a peanut into his mouth, then began to chew... "All of you who couldn't be bothered to turn up tonight are missing out on something really fantastic: the first chance in the history of the country to see a perfect game. You've no idea what you're missing."

It was the top of the seventh: the fateful inning. San Fernando was batting. The first man walked, but then was picked off trying to steal. The second hit the ball straight back at the pitcher. The third was struck out. The game was fast and furious.

Now it was Boer's turn to bat in the lucky seventh. His boy would have to take on the big guns, who were bound to make him squirm. The seventh inning: the one for the stretch, for surprises and scares. Everyone sweating with anticipation.

He was trembling, in the grip of a fever despite the heat. He looked back painfully to see the gap-tooth's expression, but the man was sitting silently and seemed miles away, all his attention turned to the radio. Sucre Frech's voice was lost in a crackle of static on the warm breeze.

The umpire's shout was real, tangible. "Strike three!" His boy had struck out the first batter.

"That beanpole is hurling rocks out there," the man behind muttered, his chin cupped in his hands as though he were praying.

He caught sight of the ball floating gently up into the white light. The leftfielder raced down the line to get under it...got into position...waited...caught the ball! The second out. The woman slapped her knees excitedly. "That's the way, that's the way!" The stands appeared back-to-front in the thick pebbles of her glasses. The fat man kept on chewing air without a word.

The first ball was too high. The gap-tooth stood up as though to stretch his legs, but nobody was fooled. A foul off to the back. Strike one.

That made it one and one. Another foul. One and two. The field stretched out, calm and peaceful. The outfielders stood motionless halfway back to the fence. A truck rumbled in the distance along the South Highway.

Another foul to the back—three in a row. The batter

wouldn't give up. "Strike!" The ball sped right down the middle. The batter didn't even have time to react, and stood there with his bat still aloft. End of the seventh inning!

A ripple of applause, like the rustle of dry leaves. The clapping drifted slowly up to him in the deserted stand. He laughed out loud, knowing that all of them in the group around him, even gap-tooth and the fat man, were as pleased as he was.

"This is a great moment," the fat man declared. "I wouldn't have missed this for anything, even though it hurts."

Sucre Frech was talking about Don Larsen, who in a World Series only two years previously had pitched the *only* perfect game in the *history* of the major leagues…"and now it looks as if this unknown Nicaraguan pitcher is about to achieve the same feat, step by step, pitch by pitch."

They were talking in the same breath of Don Larsen and his boy, who at that moment was walking back to the dugout, where he sat calmly at the far end, like it was nothing. His team mates were chatting, again like it was nothing. Their manager looked unconcerned. Managua was slumbering in the dark, like it was nothing. And he too was sitting there as if nothing had happened—he hadn't even gone down to the fence as he usually did to let the kid know he was there.

"An obscure rookie who I'm told is from Masatepe, signed only this season by San Fernando. This is his first time to start as a pro, his first chance, and here he is pitching a perfect game. Who could believe it?"

"A perfect game means glory," the fat man concurred, listening devotedly to the radio.

"It's straight to the major leagues, first thing tomorrow.

And you can scoop the jackpot,'' the woman cackled, rubbing her fingers together. The father felt keyed up, floating on air. He gave a mocking sideways glance at his tormentor, as though to say: "What d'you make of your beanpole now?" but the gap-toothed man simply nodded his head without demur.

The loudspeakers repeated the name of San Fernando's first batter. He reached first base with an infield hit. The second man hit into a double play to the short-stop. The last batter was struck out, and the inning was over.

"Get a move on, I want to see the beanpole pitch!" gap-tooth shouted as Boer trooped off the field, but nobody found it funny. "Sshh!" the fat man silenced him.

Once again all the lights for strikes and outs disappeared from the distant scoreboard. Now for the bottom of the eighth. Everybody hold on to your hats!

His boy was back on the mound. Sweat was coursing down his face as he again studied the catcher's signals. What he'd done that night was real enough, he was making history with his arm. Did they know in Masatepe? Would the people on his block have stayed up to listen? Surely they must have heard the news. They'd have flung open their doors, switched on all the lights, gathered on street corners, to hear how a local boy was pitching a perfect game.

Strike one! Straight past the batter.

It was the Yank's turn again. He punched the air with the bat, the wad of tobacco bulging in his cheek. Before he even realized, the kid had sent a second strike past him. He never pitched a bad one, every single pitch was on target. Another lightning throw: Strike three, and out! The

Yank flung down the bat so furiously it nearly bounced into the Boer dugout. The gap-toothed fan jeered him.

"Know something?" the fat man with the lottery tickets nudged the old man. "Another five outs and you'll join the ranks of the immortals too, because you're his father."

Sucre Frech was talking about immortality at that very moment on the little blue radio rattling on the cement steps. About the immortals of this sport of kings. The whole of Managua ought to be there to witness the entry of a humble, obscure young man into immortality. He nodded, chill with fear, yes, the whole of Managua should have been there, hurrying out of the tunnels, filling all the seats, dressed in pyjamas, slippers, nightshirts. They should be leaping out of bed, hailing taxis or scurrying on foot to see this great feat, this unrepeatable marvel...a line drive cutting between center and left field...the fielder appeared out of nowhere, running forward with his arm outstretched to stop the ball as if by magic; then he coolly threw it back. The second out of the inning!

He wanted to get to his feet, but his courage failed him. The woman had covered her face in her hands, and was peering through spread fingers. The toothless wonder tapped him on the shoulder.

"They want to interview you on Radio Mundial when this inning is over. Sucre Frech in person," he said, whistling tunelessly through the gap in his teeth.

"How do they know he's the boy's father?" the fat man enquired.

"I told them," grinned the other man smugly...a low ball near first base, the first baseman stopped it, the pitcher assisted, another easy out! End of inning!

"We'll all go,"the fat man said imperiously.

They stood up. The fat man led the way up to the Radio Mundial commentary box. When they got there, high up beyond the empty rows of seats, Sucre Frech passed the microphone out his window. The father grasped it fearfully. Gap-tooth pushed in next to him. The woman, her handbag full of money clamped firmly on her arm, stood there grinning, showing off all her gold teeth as if she were having her portrait taken by a photographer. The fat man cocked his head to listen.

"You tell 'em, old fella," he encouraged the father.

He can't remember what he said, apart from sending greetings to all the fans everywhere in Nicaragua, and especially those in Masatepe, to his wife, the pitcher's mother, and to everyone in *barrio* Veracruz.

He would have liked to add: it was me who made a pitcher of him, I've been training that arm since he was thirteen; at fifteen he started for the General Moncada team for the first time; I used to take him on the back of my bike every day to practice; I sewed his first glove in my shoe shop; it was me who made those spikes he's wearing.

But he had no time for any of that. Sucre Frech snatched the microphone back to begin his commentary on San Fernando's ninth and final inning. They were still in the lead, one to nothing. Just think what all of you who stayed at home are missing.

Again San Fernando failed to add to their score. By the time the group was back in its place in the stand, one of the batters had been struck out and the others followed in rapid succession. Now came the moment of truth everyone had been waiting for. Boer's last chance, the final challenge for the boy whose stature had grown so immensely as the evening wore on:

	1	2	3	4	5	6	7	8	9
SAN FERNANDO	0	0	0	0	1	0	0	0	0
BOER	0	0	0	0	0	0	0	0	

All that was needed was one last circle on the board, to close the last window where in the distance the score keeper's head was visible. They wouldn't even trouble to put up the final score; they never did at the end of the game.

There was a respectful silence as his boy sauntered out to the center of the diamond, as though he were leaving for a long journey. From high in the stand, his father saw him shoot a glance in his direction, to reassure himself that he was there, that he hadn't failed to come on this of all nights. Should I have gone down there? he reproached himself.

"I'm right not to have gone down there, aren't I?" he asked his neighbor in a low voice.

"Sure," the fat man gave his judgement, "when his perfect game is over, we'll all go down and congratulate him."

Ball—too high, the first pitch. The catcher had to go on tiptoe to take it. Bottom of the ninth inning: one ball, no strikes.

"I can't bear to look," the woman said, ducking behind her handbag.

Up at bat was a black Cuban from the Sugar Kings. The kid had already struck him out once. He stood there, wiry and muscular in his freshly laundered uniform, impatiently tapping his heels with the bat.

"That black's out to bust the stitching off the ball," gap-tooth pronounced.

The second pitch was too high as well. With no sign of emotion, the umpire turned aside to note down another ball. Two balls, no strikes.

"This is a fine time to crack up, kid," the gap-tooth man muttered, speaking for all the group.

The third pitch is also a ball, Sucre Frech screamed into the microphone.

"What's going on?" the woman asked from behind her bag.

"What a crying shame," the fat man commiserated, looking at him with genuine pity. But all he was aware of was the sweat soaking his hatband.

The catcher called time-out and trotted over to the mound to talk to the boy. He listened hard, slapping the ball into his glove the whole while.

The discussion on the mound was over. The catcher slipped his mask back on, and the batter returned to the plate. If the next throw was a ball, the black man in the starched white uniform could throw down the bat mockingly and stroll to first base, jubilant at someone else's misfortune.

"Strike!" shouted the umpire in the hushed silence, flailing his arm in the air. As his cry died away, it was so quiet they could almost hear the lights hissing on top of their towers.

"Bound to happen," said the gap-toothed Boer fan.

Now the score stood at three balls, one strike. No outs. Sucre Frech was silent too. A buzz of static was the only sound from the radio.

The father sat bent over, hugging his knees, but still feeling exposed, unprotected. In his mind though he was sailing off into the same milky vapor that drifted down from the floodlights, from the sky full of stars. He floated painfully away.

"Strike!" the umpire's voice rang out again.

"The whole of Managua heard that one," the fat man chortled.

The Cuban had flung himself at the ball with all his might. He spun round, and stood teetering, trying to regain his balance.

"If he does connect, we'll never see the ball again," the toothless tormentor said, still preaching in the wilderness.

Three balls, two strikes. Anyone with heart problems had better switch off their radio now and read what happened in tomorrow's papers.

His boy caught a new ball. He studied it quizzically. Still cowering behind her handbag, the woman wanted to know what was happening now. "Shut up!" the fat man snapped.

The black man blasted a high fly, which the wind carried over to the San Fernando dugout, close by where they were sitting. The catcher chased it desperately, but in the end the ball bounced harmlessly on the roof of the covered seats.

"That leaves the count at three and two," gap-tooth mimicked the radio.

"Are you trying to be funny?" the fat man had his blood up...a grounder between shortstop and third, the shortstop chased it, picked it up, threw to first base: out!

All his hope flooded to his throat, then burst out in a triumphant shout that washed all over them. Would his boy come straight back with him to Masatepe? Fireworks, everybody in the streets: he'd have to lock up, he didn't want everything stolen.

The red eye on the scoreboard showed the first out.

"Nearly there, nearly there," crooned the woman.

The fat man put an arm around his shoulder, and the gap-toothed fan was cheekily patting him on the back. The owner of the radio had turned it up full volume to celebrate.

"Don't congratulate me yet," he begged them, shrugging them off: but what he really felt like saying was yes, congratulate me, hug me all of you, let's laugh and enjoy ourselves.

The sudden crack of the bat made them all swivel their gaze back to the field. The white shape of the ball stood out sharply as it bounced near second base. The fielder was waiting for it behind the bag. He ran to one side, stopped, picked it up, pulled it from his glove to throw to first. He fumbled it, juggled with the ball for what seemed an eternity, finally held it, threw...threw wide!

The batter sped past first base. The father turned to the others. He still had a smile on his face, but now he was imploring them to confirm that this was crazy, that it hadn't happened. Yet there was the first base umpire in black, bent almost double, his arms sweeping the ground, while the batter stood his ground defiantly and tossed his protective helmet away.

The radio owner turned the sound down, so they could no longer make out what Sucre Frech was saying up in the box.

"After the error comes the hit," the gap-toothed man prophesied pitilessly.

The few photographers at the game gathered around home plate.

Another clear thud from the bat pulled him out of

himself as out of a lonely miserable well.

The ball bounced far out into centerfield and hit the fence. The runner on first easily reached third: the throw was aimed at the catcher to stop him there, but it sailed yards wide, and almost hit the dugout. The flashbulbs told them the tying run had been scored.

The second batter was rounding third base, the ball was still loose; the second man slid home in a cloud of dust, the cameras flashed again.

"Boer has done it, you jerks!" the fat man chortled. Crestfallen, the father blinked at his companions. "What now?" he asked in a feeble voice.

"That's the way it goes," the gap-toothed man behind him said, already standing up to leave.

The small crowd was hurrying out the gates, all the excitement forgotten. The fat man smoothed his trousers down, feeling for change in his pocket. San Fernando had already left the field. The fat man and the woman trundled off, deep in conversation.

The father picked up the dinner pail and the bottle of by-now-cold coffee. He pushed open the wire gate and walked out onto the field. Swallowed up in the darkness of the dugout, the players were busy changing to go home. He sat on the bench next to his boy and untied the cloth around the dinner pail. His uniform soaked in sweat, his spikes caked with dirt, the boy began silently to eat. With every mouthful, he looked over at his father. He chewed, took a drink from the bottle, looked at him.

The boy took off his cap for the sweat in his hair to dry. A sudden gust of wind swept a cloud of dust from the diamond and plucked the cap from the bench. His father jumped up and ran after it, finally catching up with it beyond home plate.

From right field they began to put out the lights. Only the two of them were left in the stadium, surrounded by the silent stands that the night was reclaiming.

He walked back with the cap and replaced it gently on his son's head. The boy kept on eating.

Managua, March 1985.